GH01090303

José Daniel Alvior was ᴅᴏ....
Quezon City, the Philippines. At the turn oₗ
the century he moved to New York, where
he met his English partner of twenty-one
years. Nowadays he spends most of his time
between Bath, Manila and a deserted white
beach somewhere in the Philippines.

Seven Days in Tokyo

José Daniel Alvior

unbound

First published in 2025

Unbound
An imprint of Boundless Publishing Group
c/o Crimea House New Road, Great Tew, Chipping Norton, England, OX7 4AQ
www.unbound.com
All rights reserved

'We're all just little white balls. . .' on p. 125 reproduced
with permission of Toby Thompson.

Text design by Jouve (UK), Milton Keynes

A CIP record for this book is available from the British Library

ISBN 978-1-78965-196-6 (paperback)
ISBN 978-1-78965-198-0 (ebook)

Printed in Great Britain by Clays Ltd, Elcograf S.p.A.

1 3 5 7 9 8 6 4 2

For AG

Chapter One

'Garden View', the listing said. It was a little studio on the first floor overlooking a lush backyard. There was a photo of a tree, slender and twisting, its tiny leaves sparkling in sunlight, framed by the picture window and the double bed in the foreground. Behind it, partly concealed, was a house with a curving, tiled roof that would remind me exactly where I was. Charmed, I booked it for a week. When I arrive, it's too dark and chilly to even open the window.

I fear that deciding to book based on the view might come back to haunt me, but the more essential features are, to my relief, exactly as advertised. Garden View is spotless; there are no strange odours on the towels or sheets and there is no evidence of mouse droppings or other possible infestations. The toilet works. There's hot water. The bed is soft – maybe too soft. It's so quiet it's almost unnerving. Does anyone live in this building? I think of settling in, but I'm too restless. Did I even get to sleep on the plane? I can't remember what movies I saw. One day I'll come across a scene or some dialogue, déjà vu sweeping over me, certain I've experienced it before but unable to place where or when, only to resolve I must have seen the movie on a long-haul flight. A walk might clear my head of the fog, so I put on my coat to explore the neighbourhood. I have time to spare.

Only a block away from the apartment is the narrow road to the train station, but I follow the stream of people marching away from it and dispersing into alluring alleyways. I find myself in a vibrant area of the neighbourhood, and the excitement takes my mind off impending things. In the lead-up to this trip I have been justifying its nature, and in this moment I realise I've gotten over any qualms I had about it. *You've gone over this before. There's nothing to feel guilty about.* In a better frame of mind, hunger displaces apprehension, so I keep an eye out for an interesting spot that isn't too adventurous.

I walk by a ramen restaurant and through the window I see a young man, a white towel wrapped around his forehead, kneading dough behind the counter. I don't think I've ever eaten at a ramen restaurant that made its own noodles. The place is busy enough to allay any doubt, so I go in and take a spot at the counter, where menus with pictures are conveniently placed. Dough Man welcomes me, and when I try to give him my order, he instructs me to place it in the machine by the door instead. The confusion on my face tells him I'm a tourist, and he cheerfully steps away from his dough momentarily to help me navigate it.

He rubs his hands together and a small cloud of flour dissipates in the air. Pressing the appropriate buttons, he feeds the machine with the money I hand him, and a stub of paper indicating my selection is dispensed from a slot. He takes the stub and goes back behind the counter to prepare my order.

'Where are you from?' he asks, dunking a tiny metal basket of noodles in boiling water.

It's always an interesting question, and I've learned to answer in context. Had I been asked in New York, where I've lived for more than ten years, I'd say I'm from the Philippines. Outside of New York, except when I'm in the Philippines, I'd say I'm from New York. Strangely, however, I answer quite differently.

'I'm from Manila,' I say. Was it because Manila was considerably closer to Tokyo than New York? *Here I go again, feeling sketchy.*

No more than two minutes have passed and a bowl of ramen, faithful to the photo, is served. I take a sip from the wooden spoon and it's piping hot. I smile to myself. I feel my body rejoicing in its nourishing warmth. As it turns out, I've been enjoying the broth rather disproportionately. Dough Man, who turns out to be the owner, shares his passion for making fresh noodles. Oftentimes, he says, the focus is solely and unfairly on the broth, and the noodles become an afterthought. Noodles are equally important. Every batch of dough is slightly different, he says, and one must know how long the noodles should be cooked. Sometimes it takes as little as thirty seconds, sometimes as long as forty-five, but every second is critical, and the difference is vast. Now having a better appreciation of the noodles, I seem to delight in them more. But however much I love ramen, I can never finish an entire bowl. As I leave, I assure him that he need not be concerned with the quality of his ramen, most especially the noodles.

Out on the street I pause a moment to collect myself. The temperature has dropped even more, and a soft breeze blows. A young woman on a bicycle comes speeding past me, and she is nothing but a blur save for her exceedingly short fringe that doesn't move in the wind. She seems in a rush, as if rain is imminent, and true enough, it begins to spit. Thankfully, I'd unspooled a ball of invisible string and dropped mental breadcrumbs to easily find my way back.

I haven't even unpacked but unlocking the door to Garden View for only the second time feels like I've been living here for weeks. I reach for the light switches as if it's second nature. I decide to take a shower, but nothing – not even the photographs – could have prepared me for trying to wash in the bathroom. It's entirely made of hollow plastic as if it came out of a mould. I suppose that makes it easy to hose down, and the drain hole just outside the tub supports my case. It's so cramped that I smack my elbows on the walls with the slightest movement. I bend over the sink to spit, and my bottom hits the door behind me. If bathrooms were sold in Poundland, this would be it.

After my shower I attempt to run the air conditioning, which is also a heater, but after some serious fiddling with the remote control not a whiff of air puffs out of it. It must be broken, I think to myself, but nothing a sweater and two pairs of socks can't remedy.

I check the time. I sit on the short couch in front of the television. Even though I know I won't understand anything, I switch it on but with the volume turned down. Moments later, just as I curl up, I hear a gentle knock on the door. It's so quiet the entire building must have heard it. I quell my paranoia quickly. *No one knows you're here. You're not under surveillance.*

I get up and open it slowly. The door silently swings, and the first thing I notice are his blue eyes, wide as if astonished. There is hardly any light and yet they shine like topazes at Tiffany's.

'Hello,' Landon says. One word and he's unmistakably English. In fact, I'd think it was a parody if I didn't know any better.

'Hello.' I let him in. He's wearing a black suit, a white shirt and a green tie with thin, pink stripes. 'So that's what you wear to work.'

'The academy requires it.' He removes his black Chelsea boots on the welcome mat and drops his black North Face duffel bag on to the wooden floorboards. 'This is cute,' he says, looking around the tiny studio.

'It is, isn't it?'

'It's as big as my apartment, only mine has sliding doors to create a bedroom,' Landon says, gesturing like an architect presenting a plan. 'And you have more windows.'

'Apparently there's also a lovely view of the backyard.'

'What time did you get in?'

'I landed about four-thirty in the afternoon and got here about six-ish.' Instead of messaging him immediately, I had waited for him to do so first, which was really a pointless exercise in playing coy. Wasn't I just on a sixteen-hour flight to meet him? But I didn't want to seem even more desperate by sending a message the second I heard 'You may now use your electronic devices' announced on the plane. He did send a message first, which I saw when I got off at the station. The crowds swirled around me as I stood on the platform reading it. *Active fifty-eight minutes ago*, he said, *which means you didn't go down in a ball of flames.* To which he added he wouldn't be off work until about 9:30 p.m., giving me plenty of time for a walk and ramen.

'I bought this in the supermarket,' Landon says, showing me a small white plastic bag. 'I'm guessing you've eaten.'

'I had ramen.'

'I knew you would,' he says with a smirk.

'Please,' I say, 'have your dinner.'

He takes his jacket off and hangs it on the back of a chair. He then sets himself up on the tall table at the foot of the bed, putting to one side a basket of brochures and city guides then breaking out a container of sliced root of something that has holes in a concentric pattern. This must be the weird diet he's on, something related to probiotics he mentioned previously. I go back to the couch in front of the television.

'Do you have an itinerary?' he asks.

'When I applied for a visa I submitted "an itinerary",' I say with air quotes.

'Then let's make you one,' he says, tapping on his phone. 'Let's see. . . You would definitely love this jazz café,' he says. 'This would be your thing. I'll write down directions for you. And while you're in the area check out this shrine nearby where you could wash your money.'

'Whatever for?'

'It's supposed to bring you abundance. And I'll order you this book. It'll help you get around.'

'No, please. You're too kind. Don't worry about that.'

'It's alright. I'd like to give it to you. I'll have it delivered here tomorrow.'

'Are you sure?'

'I need to order this adaptor anyway, and I want to give you a present.'

When Landon finishes, he goes to the bathroom to brush his teeth. I wonder how he manages. He must be used to all the quirks in this country by now. Just then I remember I've already used the two towels provided. Would he ask for a new one? When he steps out of the bathroom he looks all done and turns off the lights. He joins me on the little couch, and from shoulder to ankle leaves no space between us. My heart beats twice as fast. As if sensing it, he holds my hand tightly as we watch two anchors broadcasting perhaps the most euphonious newscast I've ever heard.

'What are they saying?'

'They're talking about the controversies surrounding the prime minister.'

In all honesty, I don't want to know any of this and couldn't care less. I only want to be in a world where I understand no one but him. The world can speak as loud as they want, can yell at each other, depose the prime minister and whatnot, and I'd comprehend not a single word. With the television's soft, blue light bathing us, I feel safe. I feel like I have him completely.

I lay my head on his shoulder and let out a long breath. This time, it's his heart that beats twice as fast. It's phenomenal how one senses it, how it develops and swells like a wave. Indeed, moments later, as if he could no longer help it, he lifts my chin towards him and kisses me as fervently as he did the first time, on 17th Street.

'I'd like to stay,' he whispers. He needn't ask yet I'm ecstatic that he has. It was what I'd hoped for. I wanted to have him all night, and I do.

Hours later, as I witness the frosted glass window against me glow brighter, the drops of rain slowly vanishing to reveal the silhouette of that elegant tree in the picture, here he is, fast asleep, lying next to me.

I take so much pleasure from his presence, his closeness, his scent – sweet, faint, almost nothing. The warmth of his lean body radiates under the blanket we share. I hadn't needed the heating after all. I'd woken up every hour or so and felt like rejoicing. The morning, however, has given me the excuse to indulge as unhealthily as I'd like to. Like a smitten fifteen-year-old I gaze at his slightly squashed face against the pillow. I can't get over it. *What is it? What is it about him? What makes him so handsome to me?* His is by no means a face that could save the print magazine industry, but in this part of the world he's exotic. He's got a petulant face, a long nose with a great bump on the bridge and a pale complexion prone to spells of psoriasis. His eyes are often sunken, and the blueness crystalline and cold. I think of waking him just to see them peeking through his blond eyelashes, an unreasonable demand that will surely annoy and amuse him at the same time.

●

Five months ago, I sat at the edge of a much firmer bed with that same desire to wake him, but the intention was far from frivolous. I had to leave the hotel for work, and he had to leave New York.

I placed my hand on his shoulder, and he woke up with a barely audible, disembodied groan. For the first time, I saw his eyes in sunlight, and they were even bluer in the day and colder in the morning.

'You'll miss your flight,' I said.

'How much time do I have?' he asked.

'A couple of hours?'

Landon curled up on his side and gently laid his head on my lap. His tenderness took me by surprise. Up to that point he had shown nothing but brazen desire, which was certainly not unwelcome, but I had already decided I wouldn't like him come morning. Instinctively, in response, I stroked his dark blond hair. There must've been something about the simultaneous sensation of his hair between my fingers and his warm breath on my lap. I couldn't deny that I still liked him, if not more. And I thought, *I want this moment to last forever.* I wanted to capture and hang on to that moment like catching a firefly with bare hands. How absurd – how can one possibly keep it? I took comfort in the fact that the ability to determine, at that very instance, that the moment *was* special, was a gift. Or sometimes, a curse, especially when relinquishing to the practicalities of life.

'I'm going to clean my manky mouth,' he said. 'So I can kiss you.'

He got up, and within an hour he had showered and packed. He had been so proud to have brought so little for a two-week trip, pointing out he didn't need a suitcase but a mere bike bag, where he still found room for a hundred dollars' worth of cheese.

'Is there no cheese where you live?' I had asked.

'I'm English like that!'

A quick checkout and we were stood outside on the sidewalk.

'I'm in desperate need of coffee,' I said.

'So am I.'

We went inside the big corner café below the hotel, but it was under siege by the East Villagers, who had laptops instead of flaming torches.

'This is exactly why I've never been to this place,' I said.

'Okay, café hunter. Do your thing.'

'You're mocking me.'

In the unusually warm November morning, we walked down First Avenue then made a right on 5th Street, onto a block lined with trees that for some reason held on to their foliage. It was almost lovely, if not for the massive precinct halfway down, which somehow, ironically, attracted vagrants to loiter on the park benches across it as if begging to be arrested. But that's part of the East Village charm, like the small Japanese hair salons, sweater shops for dogs, vinyl record stores with faint Gerry Mulligan coming from within, and just before hitting Second Avenue, a snug café dwarfed by an enormous tree whose roots have lifted and cracked the sidewalk.

'Australian-Argentinian coffee,' he said. 'What an unusual combination.'

He could have been describing us. The usual barista, Danny with the shaggy haircut, was at the counter.

'Heeey,' Danny said, in a way that suggested to me he was in a rock band. 'What can I get for you?' After briefly conferring, we decided on cappuccinos and croissants. 'I'll serve them when they're ready.'

We were happy to be spared the stress and pressure that went with a frantic morning coffee run. Landon was amazed that Danny didn't ask for our names to be hastily scribbled and misspelled on paper cups. We took the lone free table, a miracle considering the hour. I let him sit against the brick wall mottled with shadows from the tree. The bricks brought out the redness of his tousled and slightly damp hair that I thought was simply dark blond.

'I get it,' he said, looking around the café. 'I get what you do.'

'You like it?' There was nothing special in the décor other than being classic. Bricks, tin ceilings and surreptitiousness.

'It's lovely,' he said. 'Is this one of your finds?'

'Yes, but I've never posted about it.'

'Why is that?'

'It's so perfect I want to keep it to myself.'

'So what's the criteria for the perfect coffee shop?' Landon asked, very much intrigued.

'Well, there's three main qualities I look for. One, it's not part of a chain.'

'It has to be unique,' Landon said, staring at me dead on. 'One of a kind. Maybe even quirky.'

'Absolutely. It's new. It's exciting. Nothing like you've tried before.'

'I understand. What's the second?'

'No one you know knows about it.'

'Ah. It's just between you and the coffee shop then. I can keep a secret.'

'Surreptitiousness is important, you see. Keeping it to yourself makes it special.'

Danny came to serve the coffee and pastries, and I dove straight into the cup like a Chinese Olympic athlete. It was so strong I could sense digestive acids rising to my throat by the time I consumed it entirely. Meanwhile, with much apprehension, Landon gingerly held his cup, bringing it to his puckered-up lips. He blew over the rim a couple of times in an attempt to sip. He had barely taken one before he gently placed the cup down. He noticed the puzzlement on my face. 'I have to let it cool,' he said.

'It's not that hot.'

'I have cat's tongue,' he said.

'A cat's what?'

'I can't handle hot. When I have ramen with my friends, I'm always the last to finish. When they're done, I'm still darting my tongue on the little spoon,' he said, demonstrating the act as if he were a very old man. I laughed, spraying a confetti of croissant into the air. Landon, in turn, laughed at me. 'This is why I rarely have ramen.'

'Oh, but I love ramen.'

'I'm like that cat,' he said, pointing to a Buzzelli painting on the wall behind me. I turned around to see a blue-eyed, orange tabby sticking its tongue out. The cat was as big as a cruise ship and standing on its hind legs in choppy seas, holding a sailboat in its paw while an annoyed octopus looked up at him.

'He's got cat's tongue, just like you.'

'Well, that's because he *is* a cat.'

'True, but I guess all animals have cat's tongue. I can't imagine any of them liking hot food.'

'Yeah, I wonder why that is. Maybe because animals don't know how to blow.'

'Which explains why you never see them have birthday parties.'

'You mean in relation to blowing candles on cakes?'

I nodded laughing, unable to keep the absurd conversation going. He made several more attempts to sip, with no success, and it tortured him that he couldn't even get his lips near the coffee he so desperately wanted. By the time he was able to get past the foam I was in hysterics.

For a one-night stand, breakfast was much too fond – was it even part of the programme? I was old enough to know, however, this whole thing meant nothing even though our farewell felt otherwise.

'I do want to see you again,' Landon said as we slowly walked side by side to Second Avenue to find him a taxi to Newark. 'I'll keep an eye on the flights, and maybe I can come back.'

'My work visa expires in the spring,' I said. I paused in a moment of hesitation. 'If I keep this job, I'll have to go to Manila to get a new visa. On the way maybe I can get a layover in Tokyo.'

We had reached the Avenue, and Landon, looking pensive, had not said anything.

'I don't know many nice coffee shops in Tokyo,' he finally said. 'Maybe we can find one together.'

I turned to him and he held me in his arms. We kissed, and I walked away without looking back. I looked ahead and went about my day as usual. I took the D train to midtown and walked three blocks west past the usual landmarks. The Ed Sullivan Theater. The Hearst Tower. Studio 54, which took me about three years before I realised it was *the* Studio 54 because I viewed it with as much scepticism as the ubiquitous signs that said 'New York's best pizza'.

Two and a half hours at my desk and I hadn't gotten anything of substance accomplished. And yet, by noon, I was exhausted. Perhaps I was hungover. I decided to take the rest of the day off. I never call in sick or cut workdays short, and I was surprised how easy it was.

'I'm not feeling so well,' I told my colleague Deniece, who, securely installed in her office chair, was busy scrolling and rapidly double tapping on her phone, faint images of hearts flickering in the screen.

'Go home,' she said without looking at me. 'Blessings.' She liked to say 'blessings', a word that was engraved on an egg-shaped stone that sat on her desk as if a mythical bird had laid it for her to hatch.

I didn't really want to go home. I couldn't make a diagnosis of what ailed me – which I could oftentimes do with alarming accuracy – and even though I was fatigued, I felt like going for a walk. On autopilot, I walked three blocks north and found myself at Columbus Circle. I decided to go for a stroll in Central Park, taking the corner entrance flanked by peddlers of Audrey Hepburn and John Lennon photographs in black and white. A foliage spectacle was under way in the park, and as I walked deeper into it, leaving behind the frenzy of the streets, I watched every step I made on the fallen leaves that blanketed the grass. Every crunch ate away at my defences, and by the time I made it to a boulder to rest, I knew what the matter was with me. I couldn't stop thinking about him. I wanted more of him. I wanted more of those moments with him – kissing in the street, stroking his hair, laughing in a café.

But was it worth it? Was it worth chasing for more? I

wondered then as I wondered long after he was gone. I wondered as the twinkling December lights were taken down and petrified fir trees with stray tinsel littered the sidewalks. I plodded through the bleakness of January and February that only New York can deliver, through blackened ice, through mercifully short days that never saw the sun, and wondered if the fleeting joy one gets, however electrifying and absolute and gratifying, was worth the inexorable comedown.

Chapter Two

The answer lay here, five months later in Japan, in another rented room, and in another random bed. I'm marvelling at how blissfully Landon can sleep under such an arrangement compared to my jet-lagged yet adrenalised self, and I think it's all worth it. It's worth seeing his face again. I find details I remember, like the faint scar across his right eyelid, and eyelashes I claimed were invisible. I find those I missed before, like the constellation of freckles orbiting under his eyes, and the biggest surprise of all, his mysterious squeaking.

Throughout the night a strange sound mystified me, like a rusty pulley or sneakers on a shiny, clean floor. It never lasted long enough for me to solve the mystery until he switched sides and turned to face me. I was about to brush the back of my hand against his cheek, but before I could his jaw began moving from side to side. For a moment I thought he was about to talk in his sleep, but instead he produced the unidentified nocturnal squeaks. *Aha!* He was grinding his teeth. It disrupts the serenity of the tiny room, and I'm amused that he should suffer from it as I do. How could I have missed it the first time?

I must have nodded off for an hour or so when I'm

woken up by another round of grinding. I decide to get ahead with the doings and take a shower. That will take some time as I'll have to choreograph my movements in the bathroom. In the depths of a sleep cycle, he's completely oblivious I've slipped out of bed. I'm not sure how long I was struggling in the shower, but as I'm getting dressed in front of the television, he finally awakens, slowly and laboriously.

'I could sleep all day,' he mumbles.

'I want to see Tokyo, too, you know. I hear the cherry blossom is in full bloom.'

He sits up in bed. 'I'd like to make you breakfast. Can we cook here?'

'Yes, but there's a long list of instructions over the sink and I'm afraid to touch anything.'

He gets up in his skimpy red boxers and stumbles to inspect the tiny kitchen. After a quick rummage and bursts of clattering, he stares at a pan and the look on his face swiftly changes from disdain to disappointment.

'The knife could barely cut my daikon last night,' he says.

'I was thinking of something more conventional. Like eggs.'

'We'll go shopping,' he decides with conviction. 'And I'll cook in my apartment.'

His apartment. A bit of a sore topic for me. I'm surprised he brings it up himself. 'Sounds good to me,' I say nonchalantly.

He dashes into the bathroom for a quick shower. He steps out with a white towel around his waist and with another over his head to dry his hair, clearly unconcerned that I had just used them. He catches me brushing my teeth in the kitchen sink, a much more pleasant venue than the bathroom. There's a look of enlightenment on his face, and as soon as I finish, he goes ahead and brushes his teeth in the sink as well. And I wonder, how long has he been living in this country, suffering in the confinement of ridiculous airplane-sized bathrooms before realising he could use the kitchen sink?

He doesn't address it, but instead brings up some other point about dental care. 'I notice you rinse your mouth after brushing,' he says when he's done. 'Don't rinse. Just spit.'

'Because. . . ?'

'Because you'll wash out the medication. You're using Sensodyne for a reason. My dentist told me this and they're right about these things.'

'But whenever I swallow, I'll be eating toothpaste.'

'You'll get used to it.'

'That's just horrible! How about I rinse once as a com-promise?' I'm sitting at the edge of the bed putting socks on, and he comes over to give me an unrinsed toothpaste kiss on the lips.

'Fresh,' I say.

He plucks a clean pair of boxers from his duffel bag and heads to his pile of clothes on the little couch to get dressed. He wears his suit again but nixes the tie. In front of the full-length mirror by the bathroom door, he styles his hair perfunctorily.

'You cut your hair,' I say.

'I did. I just let my hairdresser do anything really,' as if to say it's not his intention to have a trendy haircut.

I throw my light coat over my grey shirt and blue jeans, and together we put on our shoes by the door. We step out and I lock up. Down the narrow corridor, we survive one very steep and perilous flight of stairs down to Shimokitazawa's narrow wet streets. Though the neighbourhood is a mere four stops from Shibuya, its quietness makes it seem further than that. It's a grey day, but it wouldn't seem so if anyone heard us. We snicker at anything as we stroll unhurriedly. I had missed walking with him. I even remember to walk on his right so he can hear me. 'We can steal those oranges for breakfast,' he says, pointing to a citrus tree peeking over a low wall. 'Any objections to eating forbidden fruit?'

'Already had one last night. Or was that vegetable?'

'That was meat.'

He leads me towards the train station and the neighbourhood slowly comes alive. Before you know it, it's manic. The sidewalks vanish and, walking in the middle of the road, we sidestep sandwich boards, food racks, bicycles, orange traffic cones, and schoolgirls in miniskirts and stockings. Hundreds of store signs, devoid of the Western alphabet, hang over the street. We reach the area surrounding the station, and I follow him through passageways no guidebook would ever know. We cross a railway construction project that apparently has been going on for years.

'This line under construction crosses the Inokashira – that train you take from Shibuya. This one's called the Odakyu. They've been moving it underground. They're just about done, finally. Now you see this open space where the tracks used to be.'

'I thought they were building it.'

'No. In fact it's the opposite. It's been this whole mess since I moved here.'

Beyond the construction I see a high arch bearing the name of the neighbourhood in a font common to Japanese anime. Just past the arch we enter the local grocery store, a two-storey building jammed with a tremendous amount of merchandise. It's awfully busy for a Tuesday morning. It feels as if I'm the only tourist but being Asian I manage to blend in. Meanwhile, he's the only white person, but he sure knows his way around. He makes a beeline for the tubers, and not only does he know where they are, he knows exactly which ones he needs among hundreds.

I'm so struck by the sheer variety and overwhelming strangeness of the store that I lose him briefly. I look around and, from the eggs section, I see he's keeping a discreet eye on me. I worm my way to join him, picking up a tray of a dozen eggs whose label does not make sense to me. He selects a different tray.

'No, let's get this,' he says.

We also get strawberries, carrots, potatoes, beans, swordfish steaks, thinly sliced beef and fresh fruit juices. We head to the array of cashiers, who all wear face masks for no apparent reason. I offer to pay for the groceries, but he insists on getting them. When we're done, he realises he's forgotten one other thing.

'Ugh! I have to go back.'

I wait for him by the huge windows near the entrance. Assuming he'll be a while, I take my phone out and decide to take pictures of this incredible supermarket. There's bunting everywhere. Little origami lanterns in shapes of trees, leaves and fruit hang from the ceiling, as well as square banners displaying Japanese characters punctuated with exclamation marks. And yet, for all its visual frenzy, everyone seems to be rather subdued. I take a handful of shots, and I blow my cover. The supermarket is so local that I cause a good deal of unease.

He comes back with the forgotten item, and we leave. Just before the arch, I stop for a moment to take photographs. The cramped street has gotten even busier, and from where I stand, I can see him among the madness, a tall figure under a blizzard of Japanese characters. He's walking away, each second further and further from me, the black duffel bag worn as a backpack and a white shopping bag in one hand. I take a couple of photos that seem to foretell the end. In seven days, when this is all over, is this the way I'll watch him walk off into this bizarre world? Just as I get carried away with my thoughts, he notices my absence by his side. He seems to have this keen awareness of me, especially when I fall behind. He casually looks back to see where I am, and through the crowd our eyes meet. He gives me that look – intense, solemn and inscrutable – the same look he had given me the first time I saw him.

We could have been back in the chaos of the Chelsea Market where, amid the rush-hour crowd, we tried to find each other for the very first time. With the unrelenting stream of people channelled to flow in a narrow tube, it seemed impossible, but from a distance I managed to spot him first. In no time, like a mental tap on the shoulder, he caught sight of me, too. We had yet to speak but already it was a heavy correspondence of mutual attraction. We moved towards each other but going through a crowd in New York was very different to Tokyo. The hustle and bustle of pedestrians was rowdier, and apologies were seldom dispensed. As he made his way to me, he removed his damp beanie and fluffed his chin-length hair – a smooth move – perhaps there would be no need to break the ice. Up close and face to face, however, there was but a smattering of hi and hello. His intense blue eyes seemed unblinking, and I, mesmerised, fed the uneasiness.

'Can we go someplace where we can have a drink?' he finally said to move the rendezvous forward. A task! I'm better with a task. We stepped out and away from the hubbub of the Chelsea Market.

'So did you walk the High Line like you said?'

'Huh? I'm sorry – can you walk on my right? I have a problem with my left ear.'

We switched places and I led him over to 16th Street. We walked west to a restaurant just beneath the High Line on Tenth Avenue. I'd known the spot for more than a decade and incredibly it had lasted all the years I'd been in New York. It was too early for dinner, and even the bar, right by the door, had only a handful of people.

'What would you like?' I asked.

'I'll have a gin and tonic.' The quintessential English cocktail.

'Here,' he said, putting his card out.

'I got it.'

He took our drinks when they were ready, and to my delight, he naturally wandered out to what used to be a taxi garage. Now a patio, it was almost empty, and with the music turned down low it was perfect for conversation. He chose a table under a small tree but not without accidentally kicking and fumbling with the cumbersome chairs. A giggle fit ensued, which broke the tension somewhat.

'I'm suddenly your typical bumbling Englishman, like Hugh Grant.'

'It's not a bad thing,' I assured him.

We sat across each other and settled down. A big first sip. Then another.

'The truth is,' he said rather gravely, 'I just really want to be naked with you right now – I'm sorry. I'm being crass.'

I knew he was keen on me, but still I was gobsmacked. Normally I'd have something to say, not necessarily a comeback, but I was lost for words. I hadn't been desired like this by someone I liked in quite some time. As if to make amends, he humanised himself with personal details: he was from the West Midlands. He'd been living in Tokyo for the last four years teaching English to school kids at a posh academy. In his free time, he wrote articles for a magazine that taught English to senior citizens 'who don't even know how to follow me on social media'.

'Very interesting. I'd love to read them,' I said.

'No, they're nothing,' he said diffidently. 'They're not even digital!'

'Seriously, I really would. I'm very interested.'

'And you. I know you're a café hunter,' he said with a straight face. I knew my turn would come, but I didn't expect it to come without the mockery. 'What exactly does a café hunter do?'

'I find the perfect cafés and write about them on social media.'

'That I know, but how is it viable?'

'It's hilarious,' I said, 'the fascination with how people make money on social media.'

'I won't tell anyone!'

'Well, I don't. That is, I don't get money from the posts. I work for a company called Blue Liberica. They make coffee from a rare variety grown in very few countries like the Philippines. I'm part of their marketing team.'

'So you promote coffee shops that sell your coffee.'

'Not exactly. The theory is that when we associate ourselves with small, independent businesses like the coffee shops we pick, we also capture the market that supports them.'

'That's clever,' he said. 'And you get to sit in cafés and earn a living. You're the Michelin star of coffee shops.' I laughed, but admitted to my growing disillusionment with the city, a recurring malaise at the onset of the time change in the fall and, in general, typical of someone who has lived in New York long enough. 'How long have you lived here?' he asked.

'Almost twelve years.'

'You must be a citizen now or have a green card.'

'No, but I have a work visa, which I get every three years. It's almost up for renewal, actually.'

'And that's from your employer, right? I do the same in Japan. When I left my first employer I had to find a new one or go back to England.'

'I find all that exhausting because it's never straight-forward. Whenever it's time to get a new one it's always some sort of life evaluation. Should I go back? Should I stay home? I love New York, but more and more I'm starting to believe the feeling isn't mutual. Whenever I think of having to leave I always feel sad. I can't imagine living anywhere else – well, maybe except for London, which I've been to many times.'

'Funny you say that about New York because that's exactly how I felt about London. And I'm English,' Landon said.

'And thus Tokyo.'

'And thus Tokyo,' he nodded. 'I lived in London for five years doing shitty jobs until the opportunity in Japan came up. Of course, Tokyo has its moments, too, but work is more fulfilling; I feel valued. Lucky for me there will always be a market for English teachers, and being British I'm at an advantage. Unfortunately, I'm not so popular with the gents over there.'

'I find that hard to believe.'

'The Japanese will very rarely hook up with a white guy. My ex was an exception. She was—'

'She?'

'Did I not tell you?'

'No. It doesn't matter. It's just. . . it's just interesting. But your recent one was a he?'

'Yes, the one before that was a she.'

'You cover a lot of ground.'

'I do wish I'd met you sooner on this trip,' he quipped.

He had been in New York a day short of two weeks, and he would be leaving the next morning. We had been communicating for nearly as long, beginning on the day he won the coffee shop challenge on social media where I would post a distinguishing scene inside a café and provide a clue to its name. To prove one has found the café, he or she must replicate the photo. The clue that he cracked was

26

'lone, stray London mammal'. He figured it out and sent me a photo faithful to mine, but which was a hundred times better – dramatic lighting and all. I told him he'd won, followed by an exchange that became increasingly flirtatious. He wanted to meet me, but I kept putting it off. I wasn't really looking for a hookup. I thought it wouldn't be too much of a loss for him if it didn't come to pass. However, he asked me one more time and seemed so intent, I finally agreed.

'I'm curious, though,' he said. 'How is it that I can't come to your apartment?'

'I live with someone.'

'A roommate?'

'A boyfriend.'

'A boyfriend,' he said tentatively.

'He's away, actually. He's an actor. He's doing a play in LA. I just don't want to take anyone home.'

'Does he sleep with other people?'

'Yes, if you mean he's cheated on me. At least once that I know of. Not a fun place to be. But it seems to be more common than I thought.'

'Most of us have done stuff outside of our relationships.'

'Apparently it's rather normal. That's why we agreed to have an open relationship.'

'So technically you don't cheat on each other.'

'Correct, but if I were to sleep with someone I wouldn't want him to know. It feels weird to me. It still feels like cheating. I don't know. I've never been in an open relationship before so that's probably why. I've never even had a one-night stand.'

'Is that right?'

'It's just not something I was ever into. I really, really have to like the person, I suppose.'

'Well, I really, really like you. If there weren't people around, I'd be all over you.' Keeping his eyes on me, Landon reached under the table to touch my knee. 'Where is your knee anyway?'

I laughed. 'It's right here,' I said, moving it into view.

It was time for another round of drinks.

'I'll get them this time,' he said. 'The same?'

'Yes, please.'

'Er, what was it?'

'It's called St-Germain in Tokyo.'

'That is just so New York,' he said with a sardonic smile.

When he came back, he handed me my drink and I noticed his cuticles were darkened. I held his fingers and said, 'What happened here?'

'I dyed my hair black for Halloween. Not permanently, though. I didn't use gloves.'

'What did you come as?'

'A subtle vampire.'

'A subtle vampire. I would think that if one had to be a vampire you'd have to be all in. Coffins and all.' We both laughed.

'It's only because a friend of mine claims I look like a vampire.'

'It must be the invisible eyelashes.'

'I *do* have eyelashes!' he said with a hearty laugh, attempting to grasp his lashes with his fingers. It was the most animated I'd seen him.

Was it that point that sealed the deal for me? After all that we talked about, was it his tender confession of colouring his hair? Was it his unbridled, Duchenne smile that produced lines around his eyes making him look like a completely different person? Or was it the second round of drinks? Who knew. When we were done and the dinner crowd came trickling in, we decided to leave and meet after dinner. He had made a prior date with an old friend in Harlem.

'I really want to cancel this dinner and stay with you,' he said. 'But I promised my friend.'

'It's okay. It's my fault. I was very indecisive. I'll take you to the station.'

'Why don't we walk?' he said. 'Very, very slowly.'

Very, very slowly. When was the last time I heard that in New York? In this city we dash from one place to another, avoiding, if not snow, rain; if not the freezing cold, the unbearable heat; rushing to work, for an appointment, or simply to go home and retreat from humanity. But slow down and watch each step? It's something that I love to do, but it has become something we've been made to feel guilty about. And now someone had asked me to do exactly that – to stroll very, very slowly in the most frenetic city in the world.

For two blocks on 17th Street, we talked about how much we love – and sometimes hate – New York and Tokyo, two cities that couldn't have been any more different yet great in their own ways. How funny that if someone had wondered who lived where, they would probably have guessed the other way around.

Just before we reached Eighth Avenue, by an empty playground, he grabbed my left arm and turned me to him. In one quick move he put his other hand behind my

29

head and kissed me for the first time with such intensity that I was suddenly floating amid a multi-coloured bokeh. When he stopped, I caught sight of him with his eyes half-closed so near my face and it made him even more handsome. When he opened his eyes, he looked as if he'd been quenched. As I caught my breath, I felt once more how wonderful it was to be in this city because it was in such moments when New York revealed its magic. It happens so infrequently, but when it does, all that time you spend living in the city is more than justified. I reached out to caress his cheek. He took my hand and kissed it, and without letting it go we ambled to the corner of Eighth Avenue, where we waited for the light to change.

Walk, the light finally indicated. We crossed Eighth Avenue, strolling eastward along 17th Street. 'You're welcome to come,' Landon said. 'Really, I'd like you to.'

'It's fine. Go see your friend and catch up,' I said. 'I need to sober up anyway. We'll see each other after.'

'No way. That was only two drinks.'

We reached the top of Union Square and continued walking along the west side where the organic market would be during the day. We heard the beat of a loud drum most likely coming from the south end of the square. There was always something going on over there. True enough, reaching the plaza in front of George Washington on a horse, a big crowd had gathered for what looked like a rally for the Democratic Party.

'Did I tell you I saw Bernie Sanders speaking in Times Square? I touched him.'

'I hate him,' I said.

'I like how diplomatic you are,' he sniggered.

We slowly weaved through the crowd, occasionally running into an NYPD officer, until we reached the subway entrance that looked like a sombrero. At the top of the steps that went deep down into the maze of passages and platforms, he said, 'I'd really like to see you later.'

I heard him as if we weren't drowned out by loud cheers of 'Hillary' and 'Bernie', as if we weren't surrounded by people rushing up and down the steps. 'I'd really like to see you, too.'

'I feel a but coming.'

'No. No buts. When you're done take the 6 to Astor Place. I'll meet you there.' He had mentioned previously that his hotel was in the area, which happened to be close to my neighbourhood.

'Which exit?'

'I don't know,' I said, brushing his fringe to the side of his face. 'You're so handsome.'

'You *are* drunk.' Landon held my face once more and kissed me goodbye. His tongue went deeper in my mouth than the first time, and I tried my best to make him feel I was as into him as he was me. Never mind the din of the rally and the swirl of jaded New Yorkers around us. I knew I was not backing out of it. 'I'll see you later, my inebriated friend.'

A couple of hours later I got a message from him that he was on his way downtown, and true enough, my feelings had not changed. I still wanted to see him. I felt sorry for the friend because I'm the kind of person who picks up on these things, and I wondered if he even gave said friend sufficient attention. I told him I'd meet him by the cube that stood on one of its corners. I lived only a few blocks from it, so I left my apartment when he said he was coming out of the subway. In five minutes, I was at the cube, and I found him sitting on one of the boulders that surrounded it. He gazed at me, and even though he'd been explicit in his intentions, the intensity took me aback. Landon stood up without breaking his gaze and said, 'My hotel's just around the corner.'

We crossed an avenue and passed through St Mark's. It was bustling with activity as always, and in between one-dollar pizza shops and bong outlets were countless Japanese restaurants and supermarkets. In silence, we walked by the dizzying mix of New York and Tokyo, intertwined around each other, incongruous but interesting, exhausting but exhilarating at the same time.

Chapter Three

Against the grey sky, a mass of cables and powerlines snake above us as we stroll down the street in the heart of Shimokitazawa, and like pedestrians – as there are technically no sidewalks – they're almost hanging in the middle of the street. The neighbourhood quiets down the further we are from the station and the big supermarket, and stores become less and less practical. Sushi supply stores, real estate agents and bike repair shops turn into antique shops, rabbit-petting cafés and beauty salons for cats. We walk by an unassuming sushi restaurant with a sign bigger than itself.

'That place has good kaisen dons for five American dollars,' Landon says. Kaisen dons are rice bowls that come with assorted slices of sushi. 'In New York I survived on Pret salads.'

'No! You didn't know where to eat.'

'I don't want that to happen to you.'

Further on, at an acute-angled intersection, he points to a wedge-shaped flower shop with a barn wall made of green-painted wooden planks. A row of bouquets in tin buckets are lined up against it. 'At night, that flower shop becomes a bar. Cocktails aren't bad. For anything else, if you ever find yourself in a jam, you can always depend on

Family Mart or Lawson. Their coffee is actually pretty good.' Lawson and Family Mart are the two biggest convenience store chains in Tokyo, akin to Duane Reade or Rite Aid in New York.

'Which reminds me,' I say.

'I know. I need coffee, too.'

We've moved past the area I explored last night, and I'm beginning to lose my orientation. Further along, a peculiar store catches my eye. My instincts kick in. Unlike other storefronts in the area, its façade of dark wood-framed windows and slats mimics traditional homes. But then, jarringly, a Harley-Davidson is parked in front of its dark glass window.

'Do you know this one?' I ask him.

'No, I've never been there.'

We look closer, and in the middle of a hundred Japanese characters scribbled on a sandwich board, we find the words 'Beans Shop'.

'It's a coffee shop,' I say.

We slide the door open, and the aroma hits us with force. The counter is immediately in front of us where the barista, a middle-aged man, is roasting coffee beans in a red Diedrich machine.

'Konnichiwa,' the barista greets us.

Landon greets him back and they have an exchange in Japanese. I've never heard him speak it and I'm impressed. His impeccable accent suggests he's fluent, but he sounds shy and unsure. He tells me he has ordered us Americanos and that the barista has asked us to select beans from the glass counter. We both crouch to take a quick look at the array of metal trays labelled with their place of origin.

Landon looks to me for guidance, and I point to the one labelled 'Johor'.

The man seemingly counts each bean as he places them on a delicate weighing scale. He speaks again and gestures for us to take a seat on the bench against the front window, then goes away to grind and prepare the coffee.

'He said he just roasted that batch this morning, so it's really fresh,' Landon says.

'Your Japanese sounds excellent.'

'No,' he says, chuckling through his nose. 'I'm only a level three.'

'I guess I'll have to trust you on that one,' I say, over the sound of the coffee grinder.

Through a doorway next to the counter, I can see the rest of the café, all in wood, glowing in the warmth of dimly lit lamps. A long bar runs the café's narrow length, and opposite the bar, against the wall, are several booths. Landon points to a sign on the front door and translates for me. 'No smoking. No cell phones. No Wi-Fi. No young children.'

'What's a curmudgeon in Japanese?' I whisper because the grinding has stopped.

The coffee is taking much longer than normal. It may have taken more than five minutes to filter the coffee; I can't be sure. Finally, the barista brings them to the counter, and I pay.

'Arigato,' we both say.

With our cups, we leave the coffee shop and continue our journey to his apartment. We marvel at the punctili-ousness the man has put into making the coffee. 'So, he gets those beans from around the world, roasts them in little batches himself, grinds just the right amount for an order, and makes them in your method of choice.'

'You're going to turn me into a coffee snob,' he says with his confidence back.

'Don't! I merely hunt for coffee shops.'

'There's clearly more to it than you let on.'

I laugh. 'Is that what you think?'

'How's the job, by the way?'

'Not bad at all. They signed my papers for the visa.'

'You're staying with them then.'

'If I get through the hurdles, yes. The idea is that by the time I get to Manila I will have had the approval notice from Homeland Security, then I get the visa at the embassy.'

'That gives you another three years.'

'I didn't think I'd enjoy it this much when I started three years ago. I mean, I've always been in marketing, but I have mixed feelings about the whole social media thing.'

'It's essential nowadays.'

'Good thing I really love coffee.'

'And you can run around New York posting about it!'

'Here's to that,' I say, raising my cup. I take a sip and moan in delight. 'This is excellent. This is the liberica variety I was telling you about. You must try.'

He gives me a side-eye. 'You're teasing me.'

'I'd like to know what that place is called in case I use it for work.'

'Café Use.'

'Would be nice to go back again, sit at the back,' I say rather too wistfully. Landon looks at me and smiles.

We reach an intersection with a useless stoplight as

there's barely any traffic. I'm very disoriented. I have no idea where we are. My internal compass is swinging wildly. 'This is Kamakura-dori,' he explains. 'If we make a left, that goes back to your place.' I still can't picture it. We cross Kamakura-dori and go straight ahead. From that point on there are no more shops, and the alleys are at their narrowest. The houses are densely packed together and yet it's unbelievably tranquil. Where is everyone? We turn a very sharp corner and make a quick left at an old cherry tree in full magnificence. It's so tall it seems out of place. I'm overcome by the strangeness of it all.

'It's beautiful here,' I say.

'That's an interesting way of putting it.'

'I think you're lucky to live here.'

We may have turned another corner, but by now I've completely lost my way. Halfway down a short alleyway, we go through the low gate on the side of a two-storey house. At the end of the passageway, we clamber up a steep flight of stairs, which now appears to be a common feature of Tokyo homes. Up the steps, the second of two doors on the balcony, is his apartment.

It is, as he said, the same size as Garden View, and the reality comes into full view: there's very little space for someone who actually lives a life here. It still looks like he just moved in, which he did at the end of December. He had told me of the move, eschewing housemates for the first time in Tokyo, or ever. Framed artworks remain on the floor and propped against the wall. A small bag of rice, bottles of spices, three candles in ascending height and a camping mug sit on the windowsill just above the kitchen table. He does a quick tidy-up and dumps used cups and dishes in the sink. He replaces his cordless vacuum cleaner onto its charging station on the wall.

'Please make yourself comfortable.' He must mean the wooden folding chair that doubles as a towel rack. It's the only seat with a back. I take my coat off and sit.

'I'll just. . .' he trails off as he takes the rice cooker off the washing machine in the corner of the room and takes a damp shirt out, which he hangs by the window to dry. 'I'm wearing this later for work.'

'I don't think it will dry by then.'

'No, no, it will,' he says, rather optimistically. He checks the time. 'I'd better get a move on with the cooking, hadn't I?'

I laugh. 'Can I help?'

'No! You're my guest. Enjoy your coffee,' he says slyly. All that time and he has yet to try his.

He clears the kindergarten-sized, birch-coloured kitchen table in front of me and places the groceries on it. He takes a heavy wooden chopping board and a chef's knife from the dish rack by the sink and sets them up on the table. Out of nowhere, he pulls out an IKEA-style black stool and sits on it.

'Why don't you sit here?' I say, getting up.

'No, it's alright.'

'Seriously, it must be uncomfortable on that stool. I'll have a look around, if you don't mind.'

He sits on the chair and begins peeling and chopping garlic and vegetables. I peek behind the open shoji – the sliding doors that separate the bedroom. The closet door is open and it's full, but he's also managed to fashion a rack for clothes that doesn't quite fit. I'm impressed he has a real bed, a mattress with a frame – and queen-sized at that – never mind if unmade. I've known many people his age who haven't managed to get a mattress off the floor, much less a futon. On the tatami mat I see an ironing board with no legs, and it puzzles me.

'How do you even. . . Do you kneel?'

'Like a geisha,' he says. He picks up a purple root and starts peeling it.

'So, is this the diet you're on?'

'No. I'm not letting you eat that. You've got almost nothing on you. You might disappear! This is a Japanese sweet potato.' I study him from where I stand, his long nose imperiously looking down on the vegetables, all against soft light coming in from the window above the table, which is the only source of light from the front. It's like an absurd Vermeer. He looks up. 'What?'

'You're chopping in your suit, and that table's way too small for you,' I point out.

'Everything in this country is too small for me,' he says defeatedly. He gets up and moves to the stove to cook.

I take the folding chair to watch him as I enjoy my coffee. He grabs a large bottle of Farchioni olive oil from the top of the fridge and swirls a generous amount in a non-stick skillet. He sautés a fistful of crushed garlic followed by cubes of potato and carrot and a sprinkle of chilli. He tosses them rapidly. After they're done, he puts them in a large bowl and places it on the table in front of me, its steam rising in the air like a charmed snake.

In the same pan, he makes sunny-side-up eggs folded into triangles, blathering about them so much that I don't catch if it's Japanese or Korean or his invention. He brings the pan over to the table and puts the eggs on top of the vegetables. Finally, he sears two modest swordfish steaks, which would have cost a fortune in America. While the fish is cooking, he notices I'm hunched over the table.

'You look so cold,' he says. Mainly, I think, my feet are, and the rest of the body follows. The shoes-at-the-door thing won't work for me unless the floor is molten lava. He steps away from the stove and dashes inside the bedroom. He comes out with the stripy duvet I saw on his bed and drapes it over my shoulders. It makes me look like I'm ill. 'There. I don't want you to feel cold.'

The fish is done, and he serves both steaks on a single plate. He places a pair of chopsticks on either side of the plate then moves the stool closer to sit next to me. Finally, he scoops a big mound of the vegetables and eggs in between the fish.

'Itadakimasu,' he says, dexterously positioning chopsticks in his hand.

'Itadakimasu,' I say to him.

It's as simple as it can be. No music, no distractions, no phone interruptions. All that way, after five months of longing and yearning, this is the high. I've come looking for it and the satisfaction, the pleasure, the fulfilment, all live up to their promise. Right here, tucked in a corner somewhere in Tokyo, somewhere in its labyrinthine tangle of alleys, a mere speck in a sea of humanity, two people carve out something beautiful and no one but the two of us knows. Who would've thought the simple act of sharing a plate could be so meaningful and special? It's almost a shame not a soul is here to witness it, but nonetheless here it is for me to relish. The chill of the room, the way we eat leisurely and without our chopsticks sparring – and that when we do spar, we chuckle – his eagerness to feed me, and his delight when I eat every morsel of the meal. Well, almost every morsel.

'You're leaving out the best part!' he admonishes, referring to the dark area around the spine of the steak.

'I can't eat it,' I say contritely.

'Come here.' He leans over and kisses me.

I want this moment to last forever.

He reaches for the punnet of strawberries he had placed on the windowsill, and we have them for dessert. They're small and crimson; auspicious, I suspect. And they are sweet. I eat everything including the leaves. He's appalled.

'They're nutritious. You can eat them.'

'No,' he shakes his head. 'No.'

Landon finally sips his coffee with the strawberries. I can be certain, though, that it's no longer hot and have no idea how he can enjoy it so tepid. Coffee is only delicious steaming or iced, never lukewarm.

'I could never have coffee with fruit,' I say. 'You know what goes with coffee?'

'Cake,' he says. We laugh.

This is happiness.

'You've done well here. Not bad for your first time living alone.'

'You think so?' He looks around his home. 'I wish I had that washing machine out on the balcony, but the landlord didn't like the idea.'

'I thought it was standard to have the washing machine out on the balcony.'

'Precisely. It would just give me a little more room.'
I remove the duvet over me and start doing the dishes. He doesn't protest. 'We need to go back to your apartment by three. I gave your address for the package.'

'What time is it?'

'Half past two.' He gets up to check his shirt, and as predicted it's far from dry.

'What are you going to wear?'

'Fuck it. I can't be bothered to change.'

When I'm done with the dishes, we put on our jackets and shoes at the door. Just as we're about to set off, it pours. It rains so heavily we have to wait until it lets up. We stand on the balcony outside in meaningful contemplation.

We face the house next door, and I notice a silhouette of a woman sipping tea or coffee and watching the rain. I've always had this fascination with the apartment windows I see from a moving train, especially at night. I would see people doing mundane things, and I would wonder what their lives might be like. When travelling, I would spend a great deal of time sitting in a café and do the same with the people I see slipping in and out. What is their world like? Is this a fragment of their everyday?

Landon hands me a transparent umbrella hanging from the balustrade. We descend the stairs carefully and slowly make our way back to Garden View. We pass the cherry tree on the corner, its rosy blossoms blurry through the plastic. If in Paris you can look at the world through rose-coloured glasses, in Tokyo you can look at the world through plastic umbrellas – obscured by raindrops.

It may not sound as elegant a subject for a classic song, but walking along Kamakura-dori, almost everyone I see is

42

using the same kind so it must be the unofficial Tokyo umbrella. And it hits me. There is a joy within that tells me I'm in one of those windows I often observe. This is a fragment of my secret world that I'm letting people see. I'm one of those people in cafés I wonder about. I'm not an outsider looking in. I'm one of them. I, too, shop at the local grocery with the strange tubers and masked cashiers. I, too, live in a tiny apartment with an insanely small kitchen and fatal flights of stairs. I, too, because of some silly thing Landon said, can laugh in the rain and they'll never know why. Despite the gloom and rain and the umbrella's forlorn obfuscation, I feel I belong somewhere.

Chapter Four

'You're only a ten-minute walk away from me,' he had said after I had given him the address for Garden View. Walking in the rain, I lose awareness of the time. I celebrate the victory. Briefly, every now and then, I enjoy being in the moment; I forget I have only a week. I cease to worry about the end of our time together and the anxiety that it brings vanishes. We hang our clear umbrellas on a stand just outside my door along with a handful of others. I unlock the door, and by now I've got the shoe removal ceremony down pat.

'My socks are wet!' Landon says.

I grimace because not only do I detest wet socks, but I detest leaky boots even more. I take it as a betrayal of trust. What good are boots if one can wear them only on dry days? 'There's a mini blow-dryer in a basket under the telly.'

He finds the basket and plugs the blow-dryer into the socket. He takes his black socks off and attaches one of them to the end of the blow-dryer. He switches it on, and the sock inflates as if there's a fat foot in it. He lays it on a rug, and it looks like a prosthetic limb. There's something extremely hilarious about it and I can't stop laughing.

'You have big feet.' *And blindingly white*, which I don't say.

'No, I don't.'

'You're only saying that because you know I like big feet. You just don't want me to like·you.'

He takes his jacket off and pulls me to the bed. 'Come here!' We lie on our sides facing each other, and he reaches over to the back of my head to unravel my hair. I haven't forgotten he likes to see my hair down. It must be brighter in the room because his eyes are bluer than a few minutes ago, like they've ascertained something new. He places his hand on my cheek and lightly strokes it with his thumb.

'You have freckles,' he says. 'Asians don't normally have freckles.'

'Of course they do.'

'Sure, but not a lot. And you're very moley. You have twenty moles on your face alone.'

'Spanish genes?'

'That explains the hair.' He plays with a cluster of thick waves above my shoulders.

I smile. It's interesting to me how something that's considered undesirable where I grew up could be so fascinating to him. Bothered by the racket, he gets up to switch off the blow-dryer, and the wonted silence of the room falls once again. I roll to my other side, facing the window, and notice that the tree has become more discernible through the frosted glass. It must have stopped raining. I'm reminded that I have yet to see this tree and the very garden that convinced me to get the room. I sit up in bed, and on my knees, I unlock the window and slide it open.

And just as the photograph had shown, the tree is tall and serene, verdant and graceful, partly concealing the curving, tiled roof of the house behind it. With the window open and the roof in view, we are undoubtedly in Japan. It's almost a caricature, the way movies set in Paris always have the Eiffel Tower visible through a window. I notice the garden is in fact two backyards between two houses. I'm not sure who the tree belongs to, but I can tell by the pruning scars that its owner cares for it dearly. The overcast sky adds a melancholy veil over it, and I'm racked with sadness all of a sudden, or is it the chilly, spring air?

I notice he's been rather quiet for some time. I look back to find out what's going on with him, and I see him holding a professional digital camera. 'You take photos?' I say, mildly surprised.

'I do. I usually take my own photos when I write free-lance.' He's never mentioned any of this. He sits on the bed and takes a few photos of me. I try to keep a straight face, but I'm too self-conscious. I crack up and turn my head away. He sits next to me and shows me the pictures on the camera screen. All of them are awful except for the last couple of shots when I was laughing.

'You look better unguarded,' he says. Unguarded. I love that word. I've never heard anyone use it before.

'Show me how it works,' I say.

'Focus by adjusting this, and this is the shutter release.'

I get up and stand next to the tall kitchen table. He looks up at me with a smirk, and the right half of his face takes the light from the window, his nose casting a dark shadow on the other. I look through the viewfinder and his eyes are instantly in focus, brilliant and intense, greedily devouring all available light. I take that photo. He casts his eyes down, sideways, as if to look at his watch. I take that, too. He turns the other way, towards the light, to the tree. I take that, but it's as if a curtain has been lifted to reveal a side of him, a more complex side often misunderstood and confounded with his beauty.

I sit on the bed and hand him back his camera. He places it on the floor without the slightest interest in looking at his images. He gets on all fours and together we view the tree and the garden in total quietude.

'Would be nice to have a yard. A garden like this. I've been thinking of getting a house just outside of Tokyo. Have more space. Maybe two bedrooms. I'll get more things. You know, plates, knives, furniture... create a sense of settledness.'

'You're looking to stay here permanently then.'

'Permanent? Such a strong word. I was close to doing that once with someone,' he reveals.

It was with the young Japanese girl. I've seen the photos. They were outside a shrine in the middle of winter looking serious, she in a traditional ceremonial kimono and he in a suit with a fur-trimmed coat. They looked like a couple after the Second World War. Then there were the summer photos, a picnic by a lake, wearing silly hats, of her sitting on his shoulders as he walked on a trail. They looked so happy and so young. In fact, way too young to be buying a house.

It stings me, not because I'm jealous but because Landon has laid bare, albeit unintentionally, something I never knew until this moment. *A sense of settledness.* It has struck a chord that resonates so deeply in me. Wouldn't it be wonderful to have that in New York, free from fears of banishment? That, should something ever happen with a job, I wouldn't have to pack up and leave? It's such an integral part of my New York life that it defines my relationships.

Despite nine years together, Gabriel and I have very little to show for symbols of permanence, as if we're in two different cars driving alongside each other. It was never a we. I've never been part of a we. *We're moving to Tokyo. We're looking for a two-bedroom house. We'll try it out here for a few years. . .* I don't belong to someone I make long, future plans with, and it breaks my heart. We have lain on a temporariness that makes it easy for us to disentangle from one another.

I did not expect such a realisation to dawn on me here, or, perhaps, something I've known deep inside to breach. I barely know Landon, and it's not that I want to be part of his plan per se, yet I'm inexplicably sure that had he asked me to I probably would have said yes. I'd buy more plates, pack my bags and move to the suburbs of Tokyo just to be part of the 'we'. I feel my eyes well up, and, at least for that moment, I'm grateful he's not one to dig into emotions too deep.

'Unfortunately,' he says, 'she had such an awful taste in bags I almost broke up with her.'

'But did you love her?' We burst into laughter.

'One cannot purchase a house and fill it with bad bags,' he declares.

'That would have been quite a jump from sharing an apartment with three people.'

He lies on his back and stares at the ceiling. 'I've saved enough money. My friends are shocked I have that much.'

I slide the window to close it and nestle next to him.

'I've never even thought of buying a house. I guess I wouldn't know where.'

'We're in a very similar situation. It's tricky when you know you can't stay somewhere without the threat of deportation.'

'I've always felt displaced. Like right now I have to go back to Manila, I have to get another visa. There's always that worry, that slight chance that I won't get it, like my luck will run out eventually. I've been away for so long that I can't imagine starting a new life there.'

'Did I tell you my brother's been there?'

'To the Philippines? How so?'

'One day he told my parents he was off to Heathrow. We were shocked. It came out of nowhere. It turns out he met this girl. Online. They wanted to meet, but she couldn't come to the UK, so he decided to go there instead. There wasn't much my parents could do about it.'

'She couldn't get a visa,' I say, knowingly. Because she's from a 'low-level' country, her chances of acquiring one were next to none unless of course she was willing to be enslaved (to put it harshly) as a maid or a caregiver. These were the realities of women from the Philippines who wanted to migrate to the US or the UK for better opportunities. Lucky for me, I've received an education that spares me from that outcome.

'No, she couldn't.'

'He must've been very young.'

'He was a year out of university, so twenty-two, I think. He was young but old enough. He had his own money. There was an earthquake in Tokyo at the time, one of hundreds, so my parents were in a state. My dad called to say my mum was worried about me in Tokyo and about my brother in the Philippines.'

'Well, that's pretty adventurous of him to go there. Was he okay?'

'Yeah, he was fine. Eventually he got back to the UK with her.' He wraps his arm over me and moans contentedly. 'Draw on my back,' he whispers. 'Draw anything.' He turns away from me to offer his back. My fingertip glides slowly on his white shirt. He sighs. I make shapes I no longer remember. I must have drawn a cloud. Perhaps a leaf, too, and a flower.

'I want to see the sakura,' I say as lightly as my finger.

'I have a class tonight. I have to leave by six.' The ending I knew was coming had not been set. Until now. After a long pause, he says, 'Shinjuku would be the best place, but you won't make it. You can go to Meguro instead.'

'I don't want this day to end.'

'Keep drawing,' he says.

How does one draw out a day like this? How do I hold on to it? The greyness outside and the dimness of the room; it feels like a dream. I want Landon to tell me more about himself. I want to know him through and through. It scares me that there isn't enough time.

'I hear a motorcycle,' he says. Landon gets up and pokes his head out the door. He looks down the hallway, motionless for what seems like forever. When he finally moves, he says, 'I know he's there, but he's not coming up. . .' He slides into his Chelsea boots sans socks and runs down the hallway, leaving the door open. Part of me wants to know what's going on while another part of me would rather patiently wait. I stare at the door, half-open, neither accommodating nor unwelcoming, and it looks so temporary. Irresolute. A meditation on patience. He comes back a few minutes later holding a brown box in his arms, like a child sent to fetch something.

'I knew it!' he says, as he pushes each boot off from the heel with the other foot's toes. 'He wasn't going to come up. Can you believe that?'

'How would he have delivered it to us?'

'To be honest, the way they do things here baffles me.'

He rests the box on the kitchen table and rips off the packaging tape. For an adaptor he seems rather excited, or maybe he really does want me to have this book. He takes the book out of the box and out of its plastic wrap.

'Here you are, darling.'

'*Japanese for Travellers*,' I say.

'See, of all the books I've seen this one is the most intuitive,' he says while flipping the pages. 'Very conversational. And very practical.'

'Thank you, darling.'

'I think we may just have enough time for our favourite café.'

I smile, but I catch myself that I'm doing so emptily. While part of me is happy to have more time, I also suppress brewing feelings of petulance because our day's about to end. Right now I'm my own worst enemy. He puts his dry socks on and faces the full-length mirror near the bathroom door. He turns his collar up and around his neck he expertly ties the same green tie with the pink stripes. He secures it to his shirt with a clip, and now I notice a coat of arms embroidered on it, the kind that is typical of academies. With his jacket on, he appears more like a schoolboy than a teacher. He can look ridiculously young. We've never discussed age; he has never asked. Does that mean he doesn't care? Or does he care but doesn't want to show it?

We head back to Café Use. I'm enticed by the space I saw from the counter this morning, the cosy area through the doorway. It's as warm and welcoming as I imagined. We take the last booth in the back corner, semi-enclosed with a ribbed glass panel. He sits sideways; his legs are too long to go under the table. A lamp hangs on the wall just above us, casting shadows that remind me of wartime movies. We study the menu on two wooden tablets hinged together, and this time we order fancier coffee served in jade green cups. After the server takes away the menus, I browse through the book he gave me.

'Mata ne,' I say. He smiles big enough to reveal the gap teeth that I adore so much. I think of telling him how much I love the gap just to see if he would take a compliment that's normally deemed a flaw. But then I remember the bruxism. 'You were grinding your teeth last night.'

'Huh,' he sputters. 'Really? I thought that had stopped.' I didn't realise he'd be so disappointed with the news.

'Has no one ever told you?'

'Was it bad?'

'It was pretty intense,' I say truthfully.

'Interesting. I normally don't sleep that well next to someone.'

'Except with me.'

'That may have been a bit of an outlier,' he says with a knowing smile.

Six o'clock has come. We pay for the coffee and head

to the station. The skies seem to have cleared considerably, such that one can tell the sun is setting. We walk unhurriedly, but my heart is heavy. I don't quite understand myself. I seem to be more sentimental than usual. I don't want to leave him.

At the station, I ask him to help me get a metro card from one of the impenetrable vending machines. It's easy to navigate the Tokyo subway but getting in is the challenge. I surrender a wad of yen and watch him operate the machine. In less than a minute, a silver card with the words *mo mo pasmo* is discharged from one of the slots.

'It has enough to last you until the end of your trip,' he says.

Suddenly I'm superstitious and regret doing it. We tap our cards on the turnstiles and we're through. He's taking the new underground line, the Odakyu, to Shinjuku. I'm going the other way, south to Meguro on the Inokashira.

'Mata ne,' I say.

'Hai!' he replies. He turns around and rushes down a flight of stairs. I know he needs to get to work soon, and it's not as if I've not been forewarned of this conclusion. Nonetheless, it strikes me as unceremonious, and the sudden void left in me feels like I've forgotten something, something critical that needs to be said or done. Before I can even begin to think of what it could possibly be, it's too late to call out his name. He has quickly reached the bottom of the steps, and rendered mute by the shock of his departure, I'm left to behold the back of him vanish in the tunnel.

Chapter Five

I watch Landon disappear in the train station and a plaintive loss comes over me as if I'll never see him again. I don't like myself when I succumb to raw emotions, like those I get with intense dreams, waking up relieved and wading in the wake of whatever feelings were involved before they dissolve from memory. However, this isn't a dream, even though with his disappearance it seems the whole day that had transpired now feels like one.

I take the stairs to the platform above ground, the same one I arrived at coming from Shibuya. By myself is when I feel Tokyo's strangeness the most. The sheer number of people at any time is incredible, and yet the feeling of loneliness is inescapable. It's not the kind of loneliness that comes when you're alone in your apartment or hotel room – the respite can often be refreshing – but one that's felt in the most crowded of places, and never is it more evident than in the city's train stations.

*

The first time I'd been to Tokyo was only nine months before, at the peak of summer. Blue Liberica thought it might be good to expand our featured coffee shops, and I took the opportunity to visit Sayumi, an old friend who was devastated by the death of her sister. From the airport in Narita, I took the express train that dropped me off right in the heart of Shibuya. The hotel was only a few blocks from the station – if I took the right exit. For a large station such as Shibuya there can be god knows how many exits and taking the wrong one can set you back considerably. I've seen a sweaty tourist or two schlepping suitcases in their quest to figure out where the hell they are. The turnstile alone presented some challenges, and I got through only after the wordless assistance of a station agent.

It wasn't too long before I got the hang of it. I had to. I had a list of cafés to find, the most intriguing of which was a little-known New Zealand coffee shop in a neighbourhood called Kagurazaka. I was already near the Yoyogi-Hachiman station where I had tried a café on my list, but for the Kiwi coffee shop I had to get to Shinjuku first, which, on paper, is quite simple to get to from where I was. It was just three stops from Yoyogi-Hachiman, and the last stop on the line.

The train took less than five minutes to arrive, and counting the stops, I realised the third was not Shinjuku. It was not the last stop either. It continued onward, on to the fourth and fifth. With each station my doubts grew exponentially. The sixth one came, and to my horror it still wasn't Shinjuku. I could've jumped off before the doors closed, but it was the evening rush. The train was packed, and no other city packs a train like Tokyo does.

The train emerged from underground, and that's never

a good sign. It usually means that the train is travelling away from the city. True enough, out the window, I could see a never-ending expanse of low residential homes. Panic arose within me, and the thought that kept flashing in my mind was that the Tokyo metro shuts down for the night.

No one will understand me. I'll end up sleeping on the sidewalk.

Finally, the seventh stop came, and lo and behold, it still wasn't Shinjuku. And would never be Shinjuku. The train was heading to Mount Fuji.

'Is there crime in Tokyo?' I once asked Sayumi, who now lived in Tokyo.

'No murder on the street,' she assured me. 'No crime in Japan, only kidnapping of young girls,' she said matter-of-factly. I was relieved I did not fit the demographic.

With my heart beating wildly, I gradually managed to get myself into position in the crowded train so I could jump off at the next station, which I would later learn was the massive Kyodo. The station was so busy people spilled out of the train like a full jar of ants, while those taking the train at the other side of the platform fell into orderly queues. Despite the mass of commuters, I felt safe. There's no danger of getting pushed onto the tracks, unlike in New York; however, the phenomenon, disturbingly, is that people throw themselves down willingly and at a higher rate. As I found my place in one of the queues, waiting for the right train to Shinjuku, I understood how robotic life in Tokyo could be. It would not be difficult to set myself on autopilot every day and lose my sense of purpose and spontaneity, ultimately leading a lonely existence. It was illuminating and thrilling and terrifying all at the same time.

❦

Watching Landon walk away doesn't help mitigate pangs of loneliness I feel at Tokyo train stations, which I'm strangely grateful for. Because of my Kyodo experience I take extra care even though I'm now more adept at navigation.

I've never been to Meguro, and to get to the river I have to take the train to Naka-Meguro, not to be confused with Meguro station. It's easy to mix them up. I find myself at Shibuya once more to switch trains, and now that it's much more familiar to me, I take a moment to marvel at the immensity of this city. I find a spot with a view of the famous crossing, five wide pedestrian lanes traversing an intersection of five major roads. Masses of people gather from all sides of the streets as if constrained by invisible fences. The numbers swell by the second until you think there can't possibly be room for one more. That's when the lights finally change, and all traffic yields. The intersection is wide open, and hundreds of people beetle from one point to another in every direction. The lights change once more, and traffic takes over. The cycle starts all over again. It never fails to mesmerise me. Sayumi encouraged me to take part in it last time and it blew my mind that such a huge number of people can coexist harmoniously. It would be fun to do it again.

By the time I get to Naka-Meguro night has fallen. It's a short walk to the river from the station, and before I know it, I find myself standing in the middle of a small bridge with a throng of people. Everyone is here to see the blossom and I can understand why. The river is narrow but deep, and lining its banks, upstream and downstream, are hundreds of illuminated cherry trees in full bloom. From both sides their branches reach over and criss-cross, concealing the river almost entirely with a canopy of soft pink, white, purple and yellow.

Along the paths on the riverbanks, beneath the trees, crowds stream by barbecues and izakayas under red hexagonal lanterns. The atmosphere is so festive, and yet the breeze blows ever so slightly and thousands of petals drift into the river so placid it's like a long, black mirror. Within a few days, all these flowers will vanish. There's something heartbreaking about their transience, and I can't help but wonder how something this beautiful can be so inherently forlorn.

I've been told I'm fortunate to have come to Tokyo at the right time. Many people come from far and wide too early or too late and miss the fabled blossom. Sushi is everywhere. Shibuya will always be crossed. But the blossoms bloom only for a few days. I'm only here incidentally, but this day – not yesterday, not tomorrow – is the peak of their beauty. Today is exceptionally beautiful, and it will not be here tomorrow. We may never have a day as beautiful again. I feel my heart beat bigger, and a combination of realisation, anxiety and thrill flows through it. I try to understand myself, but then there's regret, specifically the regret when Landon and I said goodbye outside that coffee shop in New York and I did not even wait for him to get a taxi to the airport, and how I resolutely did not turn back as I walked away. And though I can't possibly think what good those untaken actions might have done, not long after that I sat on a boulder in Central Park desperate to see him again. In the same way, I can't imagine what good seeing him now would do, especially since we had just spent not only the night but the entire day together. But I am here in Tokyo, and he is here in Tokyo, and for some reason I want to exercise that opportunity. I take my phone out to send him a message, but I find he's just sent one. I'm utterly thrilled; I take it as a sign.

Did you get there? he asks as though I've fallen behind on the street and he's looking back to check on me.

I did, yes, I reply, together with a photo of the river.

He replies instantly. *That's beautiful.*

I message back, *I'd like to see you later after work. It won't take a minute. I just want to see you.*

I wander along the path, following it downstream through countless faces in and out of drifting charcoal smoke. I dodge hundreds of picture-takers, but I must have spoiled most of them. I take a moment to eat something from one of the stands and then cross over to the other side and go upstream, but by the time I make it back to where I started, I'm overwhelmed with the cacophony around me.

Sakura overdrive has taken over me, so I flee the river in search of more cherry blossom. I take a thirty-minute train ride to Ueno, one of the city's few parks that's open late. Like Meguro the trees are illuminated, but here I see the maddening side of the occasion. There's ten times more people here, and going along the promenade that cuts through the park, it feels like a migration of wild animals on a quest for more grass. The long stretch of promenade is lined with old cherry trees all at the peak of bloom. Looking up, long arms heavily festooned with cloud-like clusters of pink petals reach to the heavens, and against the dark sky, it's magic. However, directly beneath the trees, shiny tarpaulin mats in a nasty blue shade are laid out along the entire length of the promenade. The tarpaulin mats act as place cards for a group's hanami, or a traditional picnic under the trees. The hanami is held to appreciate their beauty, which is somewhat paradoxical considering the tarpaulin's defiling appearance.

I divert from the promenade and take a staircase that leads me down to a path. At the end of it I can see the top of what I assume is an octagonal temple with a green roof. Gleaming under the lights, I'm lured to take a closer look at the stately structure. In the thick of it, however, is bedlam. On the narrow path just before reaching the temple, I'm surrounded by so many people I can hardly see the ground. On both sides of the path are food stalls offering so many choices it would be impossible to make a decision. What have I gotten myself into? I only wanted to see the blossom but now I'm in this vortex. I'm not a claustrophobic person but this time I need to escape. I'm finally exhausted and make my way back to the train station.

By midnight, I'm back in the silence of Shimokitazawa. The streets are virtually empty, and alone with my thoughts I must face what I've been avoiding. Why haven't I heard back from him? Have I driven him away? There must be some perfectly good and reasonable explanation, none of which convince me. I climb up the steep staircase from the street and walk down the hallway, dimly lit with self-doubt, to my door. It's so quiet I begin to suspect the building is uninhabited. I open the door and remove my shoes. Just a few hours ago he was here with me, drying his socks, taking my picture, looking at the tree. In the dark I lie in bed facing the window. I can't see it, but I know the tree is out there.

Like a flicker of hope I wish my phone would light up to give me good news, but I never hear back from him. I ask all sorts of questions to make sense of his silence, circling away from the answers that I fear the most. To come up with the ones that feel safe and agreeable, I ask them over and over, and in many different ways, until I drift off to sleep.

Chapter Six

Peeking between tall buildings, the sun blinks like a strobe light as I look out the window of the rapid train to Kamakura. Last night, when he came up with an itinerary for me, Landon had suggested going to the small coastal city instead of Mount Fuji, which I had prioritised. 'You could go there, but there's so much more in Kamakura.'

I get off at the station and immediately much of the crowd flows in one direction. I guess we must be going somewhere important. Sure enough we turn on to the main avenue, and like a pilgrimage, we troop along its wide, elevated island lined with blossoming cherry trees. Unfortunately, today the blossoms are past their peak. They look more bedraggled than beguiling. Kamakura isn't too far from Tokyo and yet the minuscule difference in climate has made them bloom much earlier. At the end of the avenue, a torii marks the entrance to a cluster of shrines, gardens and museums. An arching bridge spans across a pond over which cherry trees with extended branches weep.

It's quite overwhelming to take it all in, so I take a moment to centre myself. There's an insane number of shrines on the list Landon gave me, none of which are in this immediate vicinity. It would be impossible to see them all unless you're a shrine fanatic, which I can totally understand, but Landon insists I find the one where you wash money. And since I'm in Kamakura anyway, I must see the Daibutsu – the giant Buddha – even though it's a bit of a hike. I decide those two should be enough for the day, then I'll find the jazz café for a meal before I take the train back to Tokyo.

Since the money shrine is supposedly nearby, I set off looking for it first. For some reason I just can't find it, so I decide to abort the mission. In my search for the money-laundering shrine, I find a sign on an intersection that says, 'Follow the arrows for the short hike to Daibutsu'. The arrows, thoughtfully accompanied by a Buddha emoji, point left. Later, I'd discover that if I'd only turned right at that junction, I would've found it.

Trekking to the giant Buddha turns out to be a good way to get distance from the crowds. Kamakura is hilly and forested and can be very tranquil. But when I make it up to the Daibutsu, it's teeming with people. Buddha and blossom is apparently a bad combination. Every other second, you'll see an otherwise distinguished person posing with both hands in a peace sign or framing fifty people behind them with a selfie stick. It's madness.

Despite the chaos around me, the Buddha, with his eyes cast down and hands on his lap in a perpetual om, calms me down. Something about its vastness, its constancy after seven hundred years in a country where the word 'tsunami' was created, make me feel safe. Nothing is that important, he seems to tell me, in the big scheme of things.

I walk about the grounds and find a wooded area beyond the wall behind the Daibutsu. I go through a gate and follow a dirt path. Only a smattering of people are interested in exploring the area, and most of them, I discover, are only there for the restrooms or the concession stand with various vending machines. Meandering further, there's a small, fenced cottage with a stone marker in front. A tall white man with windswept hair, sunglasses and black down vest is standing next to the marker. As I get closer, I realise he's looking at me. In fact, he's smiling, and my immediate thought is, *Is he smiling at me?* The closer I get the bigger his smile, and when he finally speaks, I realise who he is.

'Is that really you?' he says.

'Sebastian! What are you doing here? You said you hated Japan.' Sebastian shrugs.

❡

A few years ago, I went to see a singer-songwriter friend perform at Pianos, a venerable concert venue in the Lower East Side where many famous musicians have performed before finding success. Getting a gig at Pianos isn't exactly easy, so my friend was over the moon to have booked the gig. I was delighted for him, until he told me when the concert was going to be – the Friday after Thanksgiving, meaning no one would be in town. Even my regular tone-deaf busker bashing his good old tambourine on the D train would have gotten the gig. But hey, Pianos is still Pianos, and I was going to support him.

I got there at 8 p.m. and headed to the upstairs lounge

where the performance was supposed to be, but no one was there. I went downstairs and sat at the bar. I hadn't had dinner yet, so I ordered a hamburger with a side of fries. Sitting next to me was a guy about my age who had just been served a plate of exactly what I'd ordered. He delicately picked up his burger and took his first bite. As he did, his burger squirted something from the end and it shot through the room, sticking on the wall. Horrified and embarrassed, he made a quick scan of the room and when he saw that I had witnessed what just happened we both laughed mightily.

'I'm so hungry,' he said defeatedly and shrugged.

My burger soon arrived, and I prepared for my first bite, mindful of debris that might project from it. I looked over to him and he winked. Self-consciously, I took my first bite and was relieved that nothing launched from my burger. 'It's good,' I mumbled to him.

For his last bite, he made a broom of his last five French fries and swept his plate clean of ketchup. After chewing the broom of fries, he said, 'I'm Sebastian.'

'Good to meet you.'

'Are you here for a show?'

'I'm supposed to see my friend perform upstairs, but as you can tell. . .'

'It would be good to see something here. It's my first time.'

'In New York?'

'In this bar.'

'Oh. Do you live here?'

'No, I'm from Germany actually. I'm a pilot for Lufthansa.'

What is it about pilots? Is it a requirement to be allur-ing? I hear someone say 'pilot' and the first image that comes to mind is a man in uniform with a seduced yet disgraced flight attendant in his arms. I tried not to object-ify Sebastian because, with his dark hair, green-blue eyes and far-from-pink skin, he can make carry-on spinner lug-gage look sexy. He didn't look German to me at all, at least not in a Bastian Schweinsteiger way. He didn't sound German either, although occasionally he took creative approaches pronouncing particular words. He looked too young to be a pilot and was very improperly dressed in jeans and an Elmo T-shirt, something a millennial with video-game inclinations would wear. I suppose pilots can't always wear their hats and stripes. He regularly flew the New York–Frankfurt route for Lufthansa and was there only for the night. Despite the tight schedule, he always insisted on coming in to the city. 'I can't stand staying in the hotel near the airport,' he said. 'Whenever I'm here I have to come to town.'

We finally heard promising noises upstairs, so I invited him to the show. My friend eventually performed a short set to around fifteen people, ten of them early for the nine o'clock. After the show Sebastian wanted to see more of the neighbourhood, so we walked around.

Like many people, Sebastian loves travelling, but he never brags or glamorises it on social media the way many people do, and I like that about him. What I really admire about him is that he loves longer sojourns more. Before he got his licence, he had lived in Mexico City and Hong Kong, his favourite Asian city. He told me about the kind of life he had in those cities, and how immersed he was in the culture and daily living.

'I want to do that one day,' I told him.

'It's wonderful. I love it more than the shallow bucket lists people have these days.'

He'd been with Matthias for almost twenty years, and while he didn't specifically say the relationship was rocky, I did sense a general unhappiness about him. Maybe it was the predictability of a long, stable relationship, or he was merely exhausted from his flight, who knew. I wasn't sure of the frequency of the route, but we met now and again, having coffee here and there. In such a brief period we became good friends quickly and effortlessly, but I didn't want to be presumptuous until he said it himself: 'There's obviously chemistry here.'

By spring the following year, he flew in sparingly, and I only saw him a couple of times. Last winter he was in New York and I caught up with him. He had requested to change his route and said he now flew to Asia. I told him about my trip to Tokyo in the spring and how wonderful it was. He shook his head. 'I don't really like Japan,' he said. 'I would never go to Japan.'

❦

So, to see him here, in Japan, in the forest, behind a giant Buddha, is just surreal. There are millions of people. Millions of tourists. Millions of places to be at. And we both happen to be here. I'd like to say it has never happened to me before, but it has one other time, with a 'neighbour' I often see on the streets of the East Village, sometimes at the supermarket, sometimes at Rite Aid. Then one afternoon, our paths crossed on Great Russell Street in front of the British Museum in London. We both couldn't believe it, but since we didn't know each other personally, we didn't know what to do but look and smile at each other in amazement. He decided to give me a hug, and said he was off to Ibiza the next day. It turns out such things are possible and can apparently happen more than once, but it's still no less of a shock. And in Sebastian's case, it happens in the most unlikely of places – in a place he claims to dislike.

'I'm staying in Tokyo,' I tell him.

'Sure, me too. Do you want to have dinner tonight?'

'I can't. My friend arranged a hanami for me. You know, the cherry blossom picnic. How about tomorrow? How long are you here?'

'I leave Saturday. I don't know what my plans are, but let's stay in touch.'

'Yeah, let's figure something out. Are you with—'

'No. It's a Lufthansa thing. Anyway, I have to go back. They're probably looking for me. Let's catch up, okay?' We come out of the forest and give each other a hug behind the Buddha.

After Sebastian has gone, I realise I can't walk back to the Kamakura station area or I'll have no energy left to find the jazz café. I follow directions posted at the gate on how to get to Hase, the nearest station. I get there with no problem and take a vintage-looking green train that acts like a tram. It travels at ground level, crossing streets and through backyards. It feels like I'm in Germany, and I wonder if it's because I just saw Sebastian. No sooner than I started and I'm back where I began.

From Kamakura station it turns out the jazz café isn't so hard to find. It's nestled among quiet houses, on a side street of a side street the width of about three square flagstones. It would lose its charm if located somewhere with heavy foot traffic. Through the small foyer I enter the frosted-glass double doors etched with the words 'Milk Hall'. Greeting me is a tall, antique kitchen cupboard with a large mirror in the centre. I catch my reflection, horrified at my tired face. A bulky, wooden cash register sits on a glass display counter. On a nearby shelf sit framed vinyl covers of Count Basie in Montreux in 1977, and of Miles Davis in Carnegie Hall. The café turns out to be an antique shop as well. The host emerges from an adjacent room with a cheerful smile. 'Everything is at least fifty years old,' she informs me. I ask for a table, and she ushers me into the main space, which leads to other smaller seating areas.

I think I may have just missed the peak of lunch hour because she seats me in a prime spot, in front of an upright piano with plenty of objects on display on top of it. On the wall above the piano hangs a pendulum clock and a framed circus poster. On the piano sits an Art Deco lamp, several alarm clocks and a few children's books. One of the books, called *A ma façon, a ta façon*, catches my eye because it bears an illustration of a cat in an indigo suit, with a Panama hat in one hand and a staff in another. It's a perfect scene for the coffee shop challenge, which makes me think of Landon – not that I haven't thought of him today. I want to send him a photo, but I stop myself because I still haven't heard from him since last night. I don't want to be desperate and annoying. However, doing so would also save me from the embarrassment of having been ignored (assuming he's not going to ignore me a second time). Either way I lose because I'm letting him off the hook, and I *am* desperate, so I go ahead and send the challenge. The clue: 'whole dairy'.

But then I feel the message is too trivial and unfunny, so I invite him to Sayumi's hanami. Just as I've sent the message, I realise Sayumi – or anyone else for that matter – doesn't know about him. I'm disappointed at my recklessness and total lack of self-control. In any case, if these messages are left unanswered, he'd have ignored me twice more. By the time I finish a plate of Japanese curry, he's begged off from the hanami, and I'm doubly relieved because he didn't ignore me and it spares me from either disinviting him or making up a story about him for Sayumi. *We'll see each other tomorrow,* he adds. It makes me feel better instantly, and I'm surprised, when it comes to him, how little it takes.

I manage to enjoy the atmosphere of the café with a slice of blueberry cheesecake. The last of the hungry lunch crowd have left, and I remain with a few who've stayed for the coffee shop part. The dishes are taken away and replaced by steaming cups of coffee and tea. The shift in the air is palpable. I hear a Jobim tune, and the café is, indeed, enchanting. Had this been in New York it would've been incredibly popular. It's so interesting that, after New York, I can't think of any other city outside of America that's as, literally, jazzy as Tokyo, which might, in some way, explain its obsession with baseball.

I pay for my meal and on my way out I notice some postcards displayed on the cupboard. A black and white photograph of the café's foyer with its front door open catches my eye. Taken at night, a light fog diffuses illumination from an acorn-shaped lamp hanging from the ceiling. It perfectly captures the spirit of the café, and I buy the postcard as a memento.

On the train back to Tokyo, I while away the hour's ride browsing through the book Landon gave me. I suppose outside in daylight, I'm a little braver. Cautiously, I allow myself to wonder, to ask myself something I've been trying to avoid. I circled it several times last night but today seems like the right time. Am I imagining things? While I'm brave enough to ask the question, am I brave enough to confront it? It's either I don't have the answer and I'm making it up, or I know what the answer is but I'm too afraid to admit it. But for now, I tell myself, I'm not.

Chapter Seven

Sayumi was one of my earliest friends in New York. Moving to a different country is hard enough, and when the excitement of a new adventure fizzles, forging new, lasting friendships was another challenge. After moving to the East Village from Brooklyn, in my first year in the city, I familiarised myself with every block of every street. That the avenues went 3-2-1 then A-B-C. That west of Tompkins Square Park, 8th Street is called St Mark's. Walking around the East Village looking for a cheap haircut, I found a small salon where hairdressers-in-training did free cuts.

I walked in, and there was Sayumi working at the front desk. That was how I met her. I told her I was willing to get a haircut from one of the students, and she assigned me to a woman named Donna D'Angelo. I hadn't had a haircut in almost a year and my hair was past my shoulders. I was only looking for a trim, and yet Donna ended up cutting my hair for four hours, with her instructor finishing it off for her. I went back one more time a few months later and saw Sayumi again, but then a few weeks later I ran into immigration problems and had to leave the country.

My then employer, a dodgy businessman from suburban Jersey City, had unceremoniously shut down the business because it turned out that, on the side, he had been illegally recruiting nurses from the Philippines, among many other offences. Wanted in both countries, rumour had it he fled to the Middle East. Never mind him, but the shutdown meant that my work permit was void, and I had to exit the United States without as much as folding my futon.

After spending half a year in Manila, I finally returned to New York after luckily finding a new employer willing to hire a non-American and obtaining a new visa from the embassy. At some point I once again needed a haircut, which by now seems pretty trivial in light of the immigration saga. Nonetheless, I could not do without it, so I went to the same place, and remember an astonished Sayumi looking up at me with her mouth agape. She then greeted me with a resounding 'Welcome back!', her arms outstretched like the hour and minute hand of a Mickey Mouse watch. She hugged me as if we'd known each other for decades. Everyone's heads in the cramped East Village hair salon turned to look at us. I distinctly remember thinking as she hugged me, *When did we become friends?* We never saw each other outside of the salon. She must've sensed something had gone wrong in my life and that my return was worthy of celebration. It's always been like that with Sayumi. She's the kind of person who's so genuinely warm and empathetic that she instantly becomes your friend.

I consider that day to be the day we officially became friends. Since then, we'd get together every now and then.

She worked part-time at the front desk and during the day she went to school at the Fashion Institute of Technology and took up interior design. At the time, it had been five years since she'd moved from Japan and she had become very fluent in English even though she could never say 'Elizabeth' to save her life.

'I'm having a birthday party at Tasting Room on. . . Er. . . Eriz. . . Eh. . . I cannot say this word!'

This was when Sam, her then boyfriend, would step in to correct her, albeit with a tinge of condescension. Sam was second-generation Chinese and was born and raised in New York, and his Chinese New Yorker accent was quite something to hear. At first Sayumi and Sam didn't seem like a match; they were testy with each other, but in time it seemed to be working out well for them.

About a couple of years later, Sayumi herself had had immigration issues when her student visa expired. Our friends said there was nothing to worry about, saying, 'she's been here many years', 'it shouldn't be a problem' and 'the salon is petitioning her'.

It sounds so simple, and yet the reality of getting a work permit is a tricky two-stage process that often causes much grief, as I had personally experienced. There's an exact date on the existing visa indicating when it expires, and I'll be going about my day, trying to keep things as normal as possible, pushing out thoughts that the clock is ticking, that my days are numbered. The anxiety builds as I get closer to the date, and at the thought of the complicated governmental process that lies ahead, it can quickly snow-ball into a great mental and emotional breakdown, the kind that finds you collapsed on the kitchen floor crying.

Before the expiration date, I must have already filed an application for the new work permit, which means that I should have found an employer (if I didn't have one) who signs this application as the sponsor. But not many employers would be willing to hire a foreigner, because of the cost and paperwork involved. Sayumi, like myself, was fortunate to find one. In Sayumi's case the hair salon signed her papers with the condition she shoulder the costs of the lawyers and the application fee.

She really did not have much choice, so before Sayumi's student visa expired, she filed her paperwork at Homeland Security, giving her a de facto extension. If the application was denied, she would have to leave the country immediately. After months of anxiety and torment, her work application was approved and her approval notice was mailed. She could have stayed in the country and continued living her life, but she wanted to visit Japan, so she flew home. However, to re-enter the United States, she would need to get a new visa in her passport, which is the second stage of the process.

She scheduled an appointment at the US Embassy in Tokyo and presented her approval notice along with an application that attested that she would not engage in espionage or terrorist activities, had never committed genocide, and would not trade in human organs and bodily tissues. I go through the same process in Manila, which takes longer because more people want to leave the Philippines. Perhaps gravely misinformed on the intricacies of immigration laws, which can be a deathtrap, she inadvertently disclosed that – no, not that she was a spy or in the black market – she had been working at the hair salon as a student.

Working on a student visa is a definitive violation of the law, implicating not only herself but also the business. Sayumi was denied the visa and barred entry for five years.

We were shocked. I tried to explain to our American friends that a person may have seamlessly integrated in New York, barbecuing for the Fourth of July or what have you and sounding like their neighbour in Ohio, but this is the life of an immigrant. A different kind of immigrant, not quite like what's seen in the news, but nonetheless crossing the border for better opportunities.

I felt guilty that I hadn't imparted everything I knew to Sayumi. I should have known better. I had wrongly assumed she knew what she was doing and went with everyone's false reassurances. I was saddened to learn about it, and even more so when it took some time before I heard from her. This was in the dark and ultimately blissful days before social networking sites became an avatar of a person's existence. Eventually, through common friends, I would learn she and Sam had split up. Sam visited her in Japan once but made it clear he would never move there. Their relationship had become tumultuous anyway (at one point involving infidelity and a sobbing Sayumi hauling a dried-up Christmas tree out to the street, a trail of pine needles behind her). She was devastated. But she picked herself up, and after spending some time with family in Yokohama, found a job she loved in Tokyo.

It's been way over five years, and the ban has long expired. She has travelled to the West Coast for work, but she has never returned to New York. During my first trip to Tokyo, I saw her for the first time after many years. Sayumi never ages, and like all Japanese people except for sumo wrestlers, she was and still is impossibly skinny, no matter what she eats. She was still grieving the death of her sister Tomoko, but in spite of that, for our reunion, she took me on a yakatabune, a lavish boat that sailed round Tokyo Bay at sunset. We sat on tatami mats and Tadami, her new boyfriend, was tasked to make monjay-aki, or savoury pancakes, on the griddle using two wide spatulas. Tadami's reputation preceded him. When I came back to New York after the trip, the first thing our friends asked was, 'Did you meet her hot boyfriend?' Forget the five-year ban, the 2011 tsunami, or even the death of her sister, but did I meet the hot boyfriend.

I did, and Tadami is indeed beautiful. Big almond eyes, a narrow nose and Japanese dimples (the kind positioned lower in the cheeks). He has short, straight hair that some-times sticks up. When he does jujutsu, with a headband wrapped around his forehead, he's a manga character come alive. When he smiles, I can hear the music that's played when a person hits the bonus points in a video game. We've never really conversed because I don't speak Japanese and he doesn't speak English, and on the way to the pier for the yakatabune, I thought we were sharing a laugh at the same silly thing. He said something in Japa-nese, and not exactly comprehending what was said, I responded in English. He stared at me with a frozen smile on his face, no recognition whatsoever of what I'd just said. I kept repeating it until I realised he'd never under-stand. In any case, Sayumi often translates or simply leaves him with a task like making monjayaki.

❧

On this trip, she prepares a hanami just for me. *We go to Tennozu Isle,* she messages. *It's a place with no tourists.*

That sounds wonderful.

Let me know when you get to Shinagawa. I'll meet you in front of Dean & Deluca.

I find it so odd to meet at Dean & Deluca because, one, it's such a New York institution, and two, it's also where I meet friends from out of town. On the southeast corner of Prince and Broadway, it's a crossroad I'm so familiar with and have walked by a million times. Meanwhile, at Tennozu Isle, there's no Dean & Deluca in sight, or any store for that matter. Instead, I see two enormous baseball fields with floodlights on full. One might expect a huge crowd with lights so dazzling, but there's only the local teams. I send her pictures of what I can see, and Sayumi says, *Oh! You're in Tennozu! I'll come and get you.*

For some reason the mention of Shinagawa just went over my head, and I took the train to Tennozu Isle. Fifteen minutes later she emerges from a cab with a big smile. 'Hi! I'm sorry!' she says. Sayumi cheerfully pulls out two big bags from Dean & Deluca from the back, which throws me off momentarily. 'This is the place!' she says. Sayumi leads me through the baseball park to the edge of the isle where the Meguro River empties into Tokyo Bay. The park slopes down to the water, so we take the stone steps towards the foot of an arched suspension footbridge. Under a spectacular tree, she has reserved a spot with the official blue tarp.

'This is great!' I say. Granted, the park isn't known for its abundance of cherry trees, but the ones they have are big and lush. Best of all, there's hardly anyone here.

She smiles proudly. 'I live over there.' She points to the footbridge, which connects to the main island. She lays out a blanket on top of the tarpaulin and empties the Dean & Deluca bags. She takes out a bowl of salad, spring rolls, hand rolls, sushi and wine. It's a proper feast. There are lamp posts everywhere in the park but not to illuminate the trees necessarily, so it gets dim sitting under them. As if on cue, Tadami, handsome as ever in an overcoat and hair parted to the side, descends the steps holding a lamp as if performing some modern-day ceremony of sorts. He places the lamp in the middle of the spread and smiles gleefully, saying something in Japanese. When he's seated, Sayumi, from what I gather, tells him about the little miscommunication we had. He replies with a particular smile, tone of voice and body language.

'He says he knew this would happen,' Sayumi says, and we all laugh.

'It's not completely your fault because you did say Shinagawa,' I say in her defence.

After dinner Sayumi tells me Tadami has to leave, or maybe it's her way of saying she has made him leave. He takes with him all the food and the lamp, so she doesn't have to carry them home. We watch Tadami cross the footbridge as Sayumi and I start ambling out of the park.

'It's good to see him again,' I tell Sayumi.

'Yes, he's a good boyfriend sometimes. I tell you something, okay?'

'Yes, sure.'

'Tadami's mother, she doesn't like me,' she reveals with a devious smile.

'Oh. Why is that?'

'She thinks I'm. . .' She pauses to look for the word. 'I cannot find the word. I mean, I do what I want and I'm not the same like others.'

'Unconventional?'

'Rye, rye, rye! She thinks I'm unconventional. She thinks I was in New York for a long time, have boyfriends, and don't get married. She thinks Japanese woman should marry and have children. But I'm already forty-six! No more children.'

I know that Sayumi looks younger than her age, but I am still shocked when she says forty-six because she doesn't look a day over thirty.

'How old is Tadami?'

'Tadami is only thirty-three.'

Landon is probably about the same age, if I make the computations, which makes me older by six years or so, but he could be younger, judging by his physical appearance. I never ask because he might ask how old I am. Fortunately, I look at least five years younger and no one would guess. Nonetheless, I can imagine how it must get in Sayumi's head that she's much older than a striking lad like Tadami.

'If you can't have children anymore, why would she still want you to get married to her son?'

'Exactly. I don't understand her.'

'It's no one's business if you're not married or don't want to get married.'

'Yes! Why does she care? Like you and Gabriel, you're together for long time, right?'

'Yes, nine years.'

'It's a long time but you don't get married. You have reasons. I have my reasons.'

'Right. In our case, Gabriel doesn't believe in marriage. And I respect that. I never asked him why because I don't see the point in discussing it. I don't want to have to convince him. I want the person I marry to believe in it in the first place.'

'Yes, for me I don't believe. Tadami's mother's not happy with that.'

'Well, if you don't want to get married and Tadami is okay with that, then there's nothing she can do.'

'Nothing. Tadami is okay with no marriage. It's normal now. Many people don't marry.'

'I know many couples who've been together for a long time and never get married. Gabriel and I were together for three years before gay men were even allowed to marry, and we were fine. Then it was legal and we just stayed the same.'

'Gabriel is American citizen, yes?'

'Yes, he is.'

'He can help you with the visa.'

'He could. But he doesn't believe in marriage whether for love or convenience.' I shrug. 'It is what it is.'

'It's very difficult fixing the visa, I know it.' It's quite an understatement coming from someone who was actually blacklisted.

'It's hard to deal with the uncertainty. I've been in New York for almost twelve years.'

'Twelve years is a long time.'

'I once had this thing that everything I own should fit in two suitcases. Everything! I could just pack up and go should everything ever end. I have a few more things now, but I still feel temporary. It hasn't gone away.'

'I know what you feel. When I was in New York I try to stay for a long time because I have my life. But you can make another life,' Sayumi says with so much empathy. 'Do you think of moving somewhere else? Do you want to live here?'

For a moment I think she knows about Landon and is referring to him, but she can't possibly. I've never told anyone. Sayumi makes me think of him nonetheless, and my mind runs away freely. Maybe it doesn't have to be New York. It could be anywhere. It could be here. Will I find that permanence? Is there such a thing as permanence? All those clichés about change come to mind. *Nothing stays the same. The only constant is change.* They're cringeworthy but largely true. Perhaps permanence is an abstract thing. It doesn't exist. What did he say again? *A sense of settledness.* It's not permanence. It's merely a feeling of something like it.

'I don't know, Sayumi. I like it here. I like it now. But I don't know how long I will feel that way.'

Over a couple of footbridges, we've walked our way out of the isle, and we're back on the main island. We've reached a very corporate district, with tall modern office buildings and condominiums, and nothing like Shimoki-tazawa at all. We make it to a plaza at the end of the avenue, at the foot of a giant mall.

'This is the station,' Sayumi says.

We take the escalator to an open-air terrace where I see a cavernous entrance to the mall, and in it, Shinagawa station. It's a big one, and even at past ten at night it's still busy. Thankfully rush hour has long peaked, otherwise it would have been madness. Sayumi points to the shop on the left side of the entrance. It's Dean & Deluca.

'There it is!' I say. We both laugh. It's so odd to see it here.

We say goodbye to each other and pencil in a plan for another dinner tomorrow.

'Good luck on your visa,' she says. I know she means it. Coming from her I know those aren't empty words.

Chapter Eight

I wake up just before dawn, and I watch the light start to creep along the ceiling and walls of Garden View. There isn't much colour, unlike that hotel room in New York where Landon stayed. I would realise that morning, after we spent our only night there together, that we were in a corner room, that if I looked out the window I would see First Avenue and 9th Street at the same time, that the colours from the stoplights flashing red, yellow and green, the taxi cabs speeding up the avenue, the brightly lit flower shop across the street open twenty-four hours a day, and the huge yellow bulbs that spelled 'bean' in the coffee shop downstairs, all coruscated warmly on the walls. Or was it the afterglow?

*

Days later, I could still feel him long after he'd taken that taxi to Newark. The slightest twitch or the faintest graze somewhere on my body reminded me of how he had touched, kissed or passed his tongue over that part of me. We'd entered his hotel, surprised to learn about a discreet door near a coffee shop that I'd always seen but never visited. The building looked like any other East Village walk-up, and he tapped a small plastic card on a little device a couple of times until an approving beep unlocked the door. I trailed him up the stairs to the second floor and down the long and narrow brick hallway. His room was the fourth and last door, which he opened with another card key. He had not even closed the door when he had his lips pressing on mine. He took his time exploring with his tongue, first genuinely, then hungrily, withholding, teasing, his lips discovering every crevice and protuberance – the back of my ears, the side of my neck, an armpit, a nipple. I could tell he derived so much pleasure from his exploration, a particular oral predilection that explained the cat's tongue. Next thing I knew, my ponytail had been let loose as we kissed, tendrils of hair getting in the way, which under normal circumstances would've annoyed me. Landon, out of breath, simply stared at me.

Softly, he said, 'You're pretty much perfect.' His eyes could be filled with lust, but they could, like at that moment, be so innocent and full of fascination that it almost broke my heart.

He undressed me, first taking my sweater and shirt off then slowly pulling my trousers and underwear down. 'You are so my type,' he said, running his hands all over my body. He took his sweater off, and before removing his T-shirt, he said, 'I warned you about my psoriasis, didn't I?' He was referring to a previous discussion where we gave each other the health clearance.

'Yes,' I said. He had left his skin cream in Tokyo and the condition had acted up during the trip. He pulled his T-shirt off and raised his head in exaltation of his nakedness. And rightly so. Despite the angry red spots, his physique was beautiful, lean and chiselled – just enough muscularity to mask any hint of the scrawny boy he once was. He slid out of his tight black jeans and on his boxer shorts was a large wet patch.

'I've never met anyone who precums as much as I do,' he said.

Just three nights ago here at Garden View, Landon was just as overwhelmingly impassioned, wet and leaking, and I just about kept up with his intensity. I'm not sure how I'd keep up should it come to that again, but nonetheless I still want to see him. More than the sex, I simply want to spend time with him, a luxury we couldn't take advantage of in New York. He was there for all of two weeks and the irony was I only got to be with him one night. Part of me wants to make up for the indecisiveness and squandering, and for all the myriad thoughts in my head. I want to spend every minute I have here with him. I can't get enough of him.

But since Landon said we'd meet up today, we haven't made any plans. I haven't heard from him at all. I fear that something has changed since I asked to see him again the other night, as if now I like him more than he likes me. It's as though I have betrayed myself. I've shown my hand, and he has the advantage. I hate having to message him but it's nearly noon. If he were to flake on me, I'd like to do other things, which I have yet to figure out, because I hadn't really planned on anything other than spending time with him. As the clock ticks my anxiety builds, and

I lose my self-control. I can't help myself from messaging him. Almost instantly after sending, as if in an act of contrition, he calls.

'Whoa,' he says. 'I just woke up.' Whether or not it's the truth, I believe him. We'll spend the day as he said. 'The fridge is full,' he continues. 'Beef, salmon, shrimp, vegetables. . . I do need to take a brutally cold shower, so I'll leave the door unlocked.' He's instantly forgiven.

Suddenly everything is fine. I head over to his apartment and although it's not as sunny, it's as warm as yesterday. I decide to stop by Family Mart to get a few bottles of the fresh juices that he likes, and more eggs. I take a little longer to find my way, but eventually I'm back in the quiet, narrow alleys with random configurations. Once more it feels like a secret hideaway. Who would ever think I'd end up here? The night I accidentally ended up in Kyodo, staring out the train at the never-ending expanse of city lights, I was in fact looking at a part of this neighbourhood. That I'd be totally immersed in it was the last thing on my mind, though I realise now how much I deeply wished for it. Perhaps, subconsciously, I led myself here. I clearly remember the fear of that night, and now, laughably, as I try to find Landon's apartment, I enjoy the feeling of being lost. I bask in the joy of searching for his apartment, of the likely possibility of losing my way. I make quick, sharp turns. I get flashes of temporary anxiety. I'm careful to remember the sensation, for when I know the direction by heart, I'll never experience it again. Eventually I find the big cherry tree in full bloom and know I'm on the right path. I make one final turn and see the low gate.

By myself I have the time to take in the details, which, somehow, I deem important. It's a grey house with a balcony. It fascinates me that no one seems to live here even though there are obvious signs of habitation. In the little terrace in front, just behind a low accordion fence, I see potted plants in bloom, bicycles with baskets on handlebars, and what looks like a motorcycle underneath a silver cover. This is someone's home, and like most, a section behind at the back of this building has been converted into apartments. I swing the metal gate and it doesn't even squeak. I go through the narrow passage along the side until I reach the stairs at the back. I climb up, and when I open the door to his apartment, I hear the shower running. I smile to myself. I'm glad to be here. I take my shoes off and hang my jacket on the back of the folding chair. After I put the eggs and juices in the fridge, I look around, happy I have a moment to soak in the space where he lives. It's not long before he comes out of the shower towelling off with an enormous blue towel, bright-eyed and bushy-tailed.

'Thanks for coming,' he says.

'Don't be silly,' I snigger. 'This whole trip was supposed to be with you.'

He ignores the slight dig, and it's just as well. It seems pointless to discuss it now or get in a strop over it. We're spending time together again, and I'm getting what I want, am I not? He towels off in front of me, flaunting his naked body, wiping drops of water all over his chest. He bends to dry his legs, going slowly up to his thighs, then into his inner thighs, and into the most private of crevices.

'Tell me what you've been up to,' he says as he puts on a pair of running shorts and a hoodie. 'You went to Meguro.' He then hands me a whole head of garlic and brings over the knife and the chopping board.

'I did, yes. After Meguro I went to Ueno. There was this lovely temple.' I punctuate my sentences with thuds, smashing cloves of garlic with the side of the knife. 'I wanted to see it up close, but I couldn't get near it. It was so insanely busy.'

'What did it look like?'

'Octagonal with a green roof,' I say with the crackling of thin, dry garlic skin.

'Bentendo. It's on an island in the lotus pond, right?' He takes out most of the contents of his fridge, and indeed he has everything he mentioned to me earlier.

'I don't know. I didn't see any pond.'

'It's Bentendo. Trust me, it's in the middle of a lotus pond.'

'I'll take your word for it. I probably didn't see the pond because of the wall of barbecues around me.'

'It can get a bit much.'

Is that why he didn't come with me to Tennozu Isle? I don't bring it up. I can't bring anything up. I push away the thoughts that have been on my mind, mincing them away as I do with the garlic. He cooks everything, and there's so much food. Again, we eat from one plate, and I chase the same feelings of elation as before. Somehow it has lost some of its bite, but I suspect that I'll continue to want more in a desperate quest to recapture the first time, even though it diminishes with each attempt.

After we're done eating, he stands in front of me and

bends down to kiss me as passionately as he always does. I kiss him back, but a feeling of dread comes over me. Just when I was thinking I was better at being in the moment, a new problem arises. The frantic urge with which he kisses makes me anxious. I'm confused because I've just seen his naked body moments ago and felt a stirring in me. Now I feel a variety of emotions at odds with each other and I'd rather shed them than my clothes. He pulls me to the bed and strips, and before I know it, he's undressing me.

He takes command and exhales in quick staccato breaths as he does when pleasured. His intensity is overpowering and overwhelming. He is so sexual – perhaps too sexual – that there's not a nook or cranny left for tenderness. I really do like him, but I'm simply going through the motions.

He notices I'm not getting into it, so he turns it up a notch. His eagerness to please doubles the pressure on me. He claims he is, in his words, 'mostly a top'. And even though I'm not a voracious bottom-whore, it's the ideal place for me at this point because there's something about being taken and manhandled by him. His dominance and control are intoxicating. The only problem now is that he wants to finish me off because that's how he wants to finish himself off. We persist to reach the climax we desire, and when we do there's an odd sense of satisfaction that he has treated me like a rag.

I feel horrid for my lacklustre turn in the sack, which I'm sure is not lost on him, but he doesn't comment on it. I take a quick shower. He lends me his enormous blue towel. It's still damp. There's nothing like a used towel to make me feel even more like crap. Something has perceptibly changed on only the third time we've had sex. All the emotions I feel seem to have repressed my sexual desire, and though evident, neither he nor I address it.

But it's that instinctive awareness of me once again, when he knows I've fallen behind on the street. It could very well be my imagination, but he knows. He comes over to me, partly shivering as I towel off, and lifts my chin up and says tenderly, 'Come here.' He kisses me on the lips so softly. We lie in bed, and he spoons me, giving me the intimacy and tenderness I crave.

'Do you sleep this way?' I ask. Our heads are towards the shoji, pointing to the kitchen. By our feet, against the bed, is the wall and a thick, blue curtain concealing a window.

'Would you have it the other way around?'

'If you had a headboard, I would have it against the wall. But I'm sure you have a perfectly valid reason.'

'It might be a reaction to my upbringing.' I smile because I want to know him. I want to know everything about him, together in this quiet cocoon where we never turn the lights on. I turn to look at him, and in this light, coming from the kitchen window and through the translucent shoji, the scar on his eyelid is the most noticeable I've seen it. Vertical, about half an inch long, sitting at the peak of his eyeball, visible even when his eyes are open.

'What happened here?'

'Cycling accident in England. On a busy road. I was going fast around a curve when a lorry swooped past me. The back of it hit me and I tumbled off the road into a ditch. I hit this side of my head – and that's why I can't hear much on this ear. I had a cut right here,' he says, touching the back of his ear, 'and this eyelid. I was lucky that I missed the wheel. Imagine what could've happened.'

'No, I can't,' I say, wincing. 'How long ago was this?'

'This was when I lived in London. I had to stay at my parents for a bit.'

'In Solihull?'

'Yes, in Soli.'

'How are they? You said the house is filthy.'

'It is! I told you I went home at Christmas. So many cats. Rubbish everywhere.'

'I guess it's like that when they get old. My parents are semi-hoarders.'

'It's been like that ever since I can remember. I have five siblings and because of that I'm so sensitive to the smell of poop.'

I don't completely get it but it's so funny to me I laugh out loud. 'It doesn't explain this position, though.'

'No, it doesn't,' he says, stroking my hair. 'Maybe there's no reason. It's like when people wear watches on their right wrist.'

The accident. His parents. Five siblings in Solihull. I love this. I love learning more about him. I love getting to know him. This is the most intimate I've ever felt with him. How much further can I push? How much more intimate can we be? I want more. We spend the rest of the afternoon mucking about. I ask him about a digital blood pressure monitor lying around.

'It was an impulse buy,' he says sheepishly. 'I got paranoid one day that I had low blood pressure. I think I was just bored.'

'You're a hypochondriac just like me.'

'Would you like me to take your blood pressure? We have to make sure you don't have it.'

'No, thanks,' I say laughing. 'And what's going on here?' I point to an external hard drive attached to his laptop, which has been furiously blinking like it's about to explode. I'd seen the set-up the other day and had wondered about it.

'I created these heavy graphics files,' he explains. 'I'm putting them up on the cloud and it takes forever!' He shows me the wallpaper on his phone, and posters he's made for various parties and events. Then of course there's the photography I only learned about the other day. He could be prouder of them, I think. I'd never know he created such stunning works had I not pried. There's obviously more to him than teaching English, and I'd really be interested if only he opened up.

He fixes his calendar and class schedules for the rest of the month. I tidy up his apartment. I wash the dishes and fold his clothes. I daydream of a life with him here. Would it work? Would I survive? Can this be a life for me? How many lives are we allowed in a lifetime? I'm given a peek of this other world and feel a great sense of gratitude.

'You never got to tell me about the whole move.'

In December, just a few days before he left for the UK, he sent me a photograph of his room in the apartment he shared with three other friends in Tokyo. The mattress, on its side, leaned against the wall, a handful of boxes piled on top of each other and a free-standing lamp stood in the middle of the room with a couple of garbage bags. What was once an ongoing friction with a roommate had escalated into a full-blown crisis.

'The last six months were mental. She had become very abusive to me and my friends; constantly started arguments whenever I had them over. Eventually she wanted me to stop having guests altogether. "You got to stop having boys over," she said.' He gave me a knowing look and I understood what she meant by 'boys'. 'Meanwhile, she let people stay in other people's rooms and lied about it. Towards the end she accused me of violent behaviour. That's when I looked into breaking the lease. It wasn't up until February, but since I was the primary person on the contract I talked to the landlord, and he let me go. That was quite fortunate. But then I had to find something pretty quick. Luckily, I found this, so I put down 270,000 yen five days before my flight. So basically, I just dumped my stuff here and flew to England on Christmas Day.' He lets out a long sigh.

'Are you still in touch with her?'

'That was the end our friendship. I don't know what was going on with her.'

'She was in love with you.'

'I wouldn't go as far as that.'

'She was. She knew you'd been with a girl. She hoped. She was jealous. We all have different ways of seeking attention, some more psychotic than others.'

I want to tell him something. There's something I want to say. This is my psychosis. There's a yearning in me to say what's in my heart but I don't have the words just yet. It's just as well. I don't want to run the risk of losing what we have right now. This thing, this little nook, this secret beautiful cocoon would instantly be lost. Let me hold on to it for a little longer; I've only got a few days. Let me get to know him more than anyone; I'll take every little detail and relish it.

'Do send me those photos I took of you,' I remind him.

He uploads them from his camera to his computer. We look at the photos and he laughs at himself even though he looks good in almost all of them. If they were unflattering, the photographer's incompetence is to be blamed entirely.

'This one's my favourite,' I say. He's looking straight at the lens with the slightest hint of a smile. The light comes from the window; I had opened it to look at the garden. But the light is one thing – it's the shadows that tell the story. The ones behind him, lurking in the corners of the room, suggest rain has yielded, for the time being, to an overcast afternoon. The subtle ones all over his white shirt reveal our endless lolling in bed. But the one cast on the left side of his face, partially diminishing the blueness of that eye, tries to unravel a mystery about him that his beauty often distracts from. One can easily fall for it, as I do each time. 'You are beautiful,' I tell him.

'No, I'm not,' he scoffs and exhales sharply. I've picked up on his inability to take a compliment, and it's definitely a thing. Surely he must have some awareness of his good looks? He had told me before that he'd been to castings and had been hired for the odd modelling job, which he wouldn't have gone to or taken if he didn't think he was the least bit attractive. Could it be what the shadow conveys? That behind this undue self-effacement is something more complex than modesty? Self-esteem? Insecurity?

Loneliness? What is it? Hours ago, all I wanted was to see him again. Spend a minute with him. Now I want to uncover the shadow side of him.

'I have to teach a class tonight,' he says.

'Of course.'

'I'll have a day off tomorrow. It's not every day you get a day off on your birthday.'

'It's your birthday tomorrow?'

'Yes,' he says nonchalantly.

'We should do something!'

'No, it's just a birthday. I don't really do anything.'

'Well, at least let's have dinner. Let me take you out.'

'I'll be at home the whole day tomorrow. Mostly reading.'

'Just one drink. Come on. It'll be fun.'

'For fuck's sake. You're such a limpet.'

I'm stumped by his dismissal. There's no changing his mind, and I let it go. Why, then, would he mention it at all if he had not wanted to draw attention to it? Here lies the contradiction, like modelling with no awareness of his looks.

It's almost six, and we walk together on Kamakura-dori. Even though I have the urge to take him to Shimoki-tazawa station, we part ways on the corner of my street for fear that I might push him further away. I do, however, allow myself to watch him walk away. He does so at the same pace as we've been walking, and it reassures me somewhat especially in light of his outburst. I suppose I'm reading meanings into things a little too much. I should be content with the time I spend with him and with what I've learned about him. I should be grateful to have this day. We've already had so much more than New York, and whatever regret I have had has already been rectified. Something in me, however, is pushing me to go all the way and never hold back. I should have walked with him to the station. I should be with him tomorrow. I should give in to all the urges and abandon myself to whatever force is in control. There's no way I can run away from this. I must see this through, whatever the outcome, whatever it may bring.

Chapter Nine

Sayumi once asked me what my favourite Japanese dish was, and I mentioned a bunch. 'I like oyakodon,' which is chicken and egg over rice. 'Or katsudon,' which is the breaded pork version. 'More often than not I get tonkatsu,' which is the katsudon without the egg.

'You like this food?' she asked with a pinch of scorn, and it made me laugh. It appears that what I really like are pedestrian, workaday dishes, like someone saying 'spaghetti' or 'hamburger' or 'fried chicken'.

'I love tonkatsu,' I tell her. For many, many years now I've loved these fried breaded pork cutlets. I had them for the first time in Manila many years ago and imagined what they would be like in Japan. Where I get them in New York is fine, I suppose, but I know they can be better.

Tonight, not only is she taking me to a restaurant that specialises in the dish, but to one that's been around for more than seventy-five years. After a quick nap, I meet her outside Meguro station (*not* Naka-Meguro). The restaurant is a stone's throw away from the station, on the ground floor of a nondescript three-storey building without English signs. We come in and immediately you see that it's a huge, open space with minimalist – maybe utilitarian – décor. Taking up most of the space is a large, square open kitchen set against the wall, its three sides bordered with a bar where customers dine. It's packed and there's a massive wait. A young man in the kitchen makes eye contact with us and flashes a peace sign. Sayumi nods, and I realise he'd asked us if we're a party of two, and not because the Japanese flash their favourite hand sign at any given opportunity. We join the people milling about by the door. I notice people sitting on chairs lined up against the wall opposite the bar, and it turns out to be the waiting area.

After a few minutes, the young man points us to a couple of seats against the wall that have been vacated. There's no queue, but whenever a seat at the bar becomes available, he picks from among the seated customers who gets the spot. I have no idea how he remembers who came first. Either he has an incredible memory, or he relies on the randomness to create an illusion that you haven't been waiting for half an hour. Not that there's any danger of boredom. The action behind the bar is like a show, a smooth, solemn operation by a handful of people immaculately dressed in chef's whites.

Using regular chopsticks, the only woman in the team delicately places balls of shredded cabbage on each plate. On one side of the kitchen there are enormous vats of oil where the pork is deep fried. Another young man is in charge of the frying, handling the pork pieces, which are roughly the size of a chicken breast, with giant chopsticks that are slightly thicker than drumsticks. He lets the cutlets rest on a cooling rack where the oldest man in the group takes them for cutting. He's hunched over the counter, first cutting the pork lengthwise down the middle, then crosswise into pieces about an inch thick. There's a moment when he runs out of pork to cut, and instead of straightening up it seems the hunch is permanent. I hate to think he's been doing that for seventy-five years.

A few customers at the bar leave, and the young man who decides who gets to eat looks around the room. I feel the tension rise as the hungry patrons hold their breath. He makes eye contact and points to us briskly, like winners in a dog show. Together, Sayumi and I say 'Yes!' and we laugh as we take two vacant spots at the bar. We're finally seated, and a senior member of staff greets us. He speaks to us in Japanese and Sayumi nods. She tells me there's no menu. There's no menu because there's only two items to choose from: leaner or fatter. If only life were this easy. I choose fatter because I'm not going to eat this every day. In a few minutes the same man serves us our meal. The pork comes with miso soup, the said balls of shredded cabbage, a bowl of rice and a small plate of pickles. Sayumi tells me about the condiments available in front of us, should I need enhancements.

'Itadakimasu!' we say to each other.

I first try the soup and it's sublime. Not only does it come with shimmering jewels of fat floating on top, but it also has numerous pieces of pork instead of tofu. I've never had miso soup with meat. These days when pesto is made with kale instead of the innocent yet demonised basil, I welcome a fat-full bowl of miso soup. I next try the shredded cabbage and it is out of this world.

'This is incredible. What is this dressing?' I ask Sayumi.

'You did not put dressing!'

We both laugh that I've discovered I like cabbage neat.

As for the pork, the dark sauce that, in my Westernised experience, is always drenched generously on top, is strategically and minimally daubed underneath. This way, the crumpled, golden beauty of the crispy breading can be heralded and admired, with the tender, moist meat peeking between the slices. The old man has got his technique down. It's as delectable as it looks, and I'm saddened when I make it to the last bite. How can it go by so fast? I hate to be dramatic over food, but how can something so good end so soon? And when will I ever get to have it again? We leave the restaurant and as we walk away, I look back to give it one last glance.

Sayumi and I stroll to a café nearby on Meguro-dori. She knows I'm picky because of my job although I always tell her not to think about it. I'd just love to try where she goes. It's all about other people's worlds – as long as it's not a chain. It's not, and apparently this café has been around since 1952. We climb several steps up from the street and enter, and the first thing I notice is that the wall on one side has three huge Audrey Hepburn posters. One is an original poster of *Roman Holiday*, and another, on the far end, is *Breakfast at Tiffany's*. Between the two is a blown-up black and white photograph of Audrey with her gloved fists under her chin. I love it already, I suppose.

Because it's late, the café is empty, and it's probably for the best. My nose picks up a lingering cigarette odour, so it's most likely a smoking café, which is in keeping with its original dark wood furnishings. It's almost entirely sectioned in booths, all in the same dark wood, and the tables and chairs are slightly battered and scraped. This café is a snapshot of its time, and I can imagine it when it had just opened in 1952, except the walls would be empty because in Italy, Audrey Hepburn was still filming *Roman Holiday*. Sayumi and I choose to forgo the booths for a round table at the front. The glass storefront is zigzagged, creating little nooks with a vista of the vibrant avenue. We order café mélange, which is basically black coffee with a generous dollop of double cream. Stuffed with tonkatsu, we decide against the famed strawberry torte.

'How's Tadami? I'm sorry he couldn't come.'

'He is a. . . seeing his mom.'

'Oh.'

'Yes. She hates me,' Sayumi says with a loud giggle. 'But Tadami, he's a little like his mom.'

'What do you mean?'

'Tadami comes from a very good family. It's a traditional family. He went to a very good school. Very expensive school.'

'Oh, right. But not many people can say they went to FIT,' I say in Sayumi's defence.

'No, but this is Japanese society. Very traditional. All of them go to this school. Sometimes the same attitudes. Sometimes not nice. There is a kind of wife for them.'

And it's true that Sayumi is far from the usual traditional Japanese wife, should she ever be married. She's very independent. She left her country for New York, lived by herself and relied on herself. She had romances with men who had no idea of traditional Japanese relationships, and she loved it. Sayumi was proactive about leaving them when she knew the end was nigh, although she does seem to gravitate towards a particular type. There was superior Sam, of course, who was condescending and who cheated on her. After settling back in Tokyo, she was with mad Kojiro, who, one day, packed all their kitchen knives, took the Shinkansen to Osaka and was never heard from again. There may be a couple more in between that I don't know about. Then there is Tadami, whose empathy – or lack thereof – is what he has inherited from his mother the most.

Sayumi tells me of the time when her sister Tomoko's health had started to fail. I never got the full story because we had little communication at the time. She says she and Tomoko had become close when she resettled in Tokyo after the visa fiasco. I remember receiving a Christmas card once, a photo of the two of them with the greeting *Merry Christmas and have a nice day!* It was signed, *Love from Sayumi and my sister Tomoko.*

'When Tomoko was diagnosed with cancer, I was very worried. I did everything to help her. We went to chemotherapy, but it was very expensive. It was thousands and thousands of dollars.'

Soon it had become clear that Tomoko wasn't going to get well. The doctor told her there was no hope, so Sayumi packed her bags and drove down to Kamakura for their favourite thing: walks on the beach. Weak but undeniably happy, Tomoko tried her best to enjoy the sun and the wet sand. They did that every day until she was too weak to walk, and then she died.

'I was very sad. I miss her. But Tadami was not very nice,' Sayumi says. 'He said, "Just get a dog!" How very mean! Replace my sister with a dog!' She is almost in tears.

It might be accurate to say that Tadami wasn't exactly the most supportive of partners at such a sorrowful period in her life. It's quite telling about Tadami, but Sayumi too, in that she does have a penchant for men with a streak of meanness in them. I can't be certain, but she may be aware and does in fact look for this quality in men. I suppose most people have inclinations for their preferred kind of lover, and it makes me wonder if I have a few of my own that aren't exactly healthy. Could Landon be just another link in a chain of a certain kind of man?

I feel the urge to tell Sayumi about Landon and share this experience unfolding in her city, how beautiful it is, how confusing, and to simply bear witness. That there would be at least one person in the world who I can talk to, when I look back one day, about that time in Tokyo thirty, forty, even fifty springs ago. But I stop myself. I don't know why. If it were said out loud, would it make it real? Would it cease to be this dreamworld? Would I see truths I didn't want to recognise? Would I come to realise that I take pleasure gobbling up every breadcrumb Landon flings at me to feed an addiction to longing? Or perhaps, more frighteningly, that deep down, I like all *this* – the displacement and the unsettledness. There's a fear in me to learn something about myself, to learn my truest and unhealthiest proclivities. I've not examined my life that deeply yet, and in any case, it would be hard to see from here, surrounded by Tokyo's beauty. This isn't the right time. I don't want to know if this is something I shouldn't have done, that knowing Landon and being here is, despite all the joy, just part of a series of mistakes.

In spite of their issues and the occasional maternal

intrusions, Sayumi and Tadami seem to be just fine. That Tadami doesn't mind having Tomoko's urn in the living room, for now, is a promising sign. In the works is a trip to London to visit Tomoko's closest friends. At the end of the night, before we go our separate ways, I ask her for some recommendations.

'Where do you think I can buy nice plates? I need to get some for a friend.' It's the closest I get to telling her about Landon.

Chapter Ten

The last time I was in Shinjuku station I had to abandon my plans. In my quest to find the New Zealand café in Kagurazaka, I had to make a transfer at the station. But after going in the opposite direction and ending up in Kyodo, I finally made it, fairly traumatised. Shinjuku turned out to be scarier than Kyodo. It was so massive I couldn't find my way around. To make matters worse, I had chosen a particularly bad time to be there – rush hour. The station is already busy as it is; I don't think it ever really quiets down. Fresh from my Kyodo experience my confidence was at a low point. I was so confused and beaten, I called it a day and went back to my hotel bleary eyed.

This time around, I want to go to Shinjuku Gyoen, a park so close to the station it couldn't be more convenient. Apparently, it's five stops away from my neighbourhood and only takes nine minutes, according to the map. Nevertheless, I make sure to go over my research twice and charge up my pocket Wi-Fi just in case I accidentally take the train to Mount Fuji again. Another thing to note – I'm not looking for a train transfer but an exit, and the station allegedly has 200 exits. *200*. That's not a train station. That's an airport. No subway station in New York comes close to this. None of them. Sometimes, at Grand Central Terminal, I'll end up on Lexington instead of 42nd Street, but that's okay. That's only around the corner. At Shinjuku, if you take exit 1 instead of 199, you're in a great deal of trouble.

I wonder if there's a train god because, by some miracle, I manage to find the correct exit. It should be a ten-minute walk to the park's entrance, and on the ninth minute, the daunting, hectic street levels out to reveal the tops of tall cherry trees. The park really is a short walk from there. A small crowd has gathered at the gate, which promptly opens at 9 a.m. After paying a small fee at the booth, I march inside with the crowd somewhat ceremoniously, perhaps because to some extent we're aware of desecrating the place. The crowd disperses to different parts of the park, and I find myself on a wide-open lawn bordered by cherry trees that look like fluffy, pink clouds on sticks. They block out the city from view, except for a tower sticking out that reminds me of the Empire State Building. I don't know what to do with myself. In any direction I look, the blossom is everywhere. I'm living in a painting.

It's a bright, sunny day with no need for a coat. By the time I make it to the middle of the park, a large group of people in very minimal athletic gear precariously hold the crescent lunge pose, their arms outstretched to the sky as if catching a baby from a burning building. It's a spectacular sight. I wander into the forest of cherry trees. In the thick of it, under the canopy of the blossom, I'm sheltered by what seems like an enormous embroidery of flowers in soft pink, interrupted by black jagged trunks and branches.

The effect is like a broken mirror. I see a mother and her preschool son twirling together in absolute glee as petals drizzle from above. The scene pretty much sums up my feelings for it. Within a couple of hours, the crowd has swelled considerably, and the madness has begun. It's time to leave. This is perhaps the best way to enjoy the sakura: on your own terms.

Sayumi had recommended a couple of places to buy plates, so I take the train back to Shibuya. She had first suggested a place called Loft, and then perhaps Tokyu Hands. I'd been to both places before, but Tokyu Hands was particularly memorable. It's a veritable collection of goods and has everything you can possibly imagine, and because of the sheer amount and oddness of merchandise, it's become quite the tourist attraction. They sell books, records, water pipes, sushi-moulding apparatus, toe socks, ice cream, ramen and fried chicken, among a million other random things. At the pet section, one can purchase live and electronic pets. On multiple levels, it can be over-whelming, sometimes even annoying, and one may have to make multiple visits. I can't think of an equivalent in New York other than the Met Museum.

But the joke's on me. I search and search and despite the selection I don't find anything I think Landon would like. I realise how little I know him. In fact, I don't know him at all.

I take Sayumi's first recommendation and head to Loft. Loft is more like Crate & Barrel, or maybe West Elm, depending on your perspective. There the task is more straightforward, and I find off-white plates that would go well with his existing ones. I don't buy more than four because that kindergarten table that he has can't possibly seat more than four people anyway. I get a few pieces of silverware to go along with the plates.

Back at Garden View, I decide to give him the postcard I got at Milk Hall even though I want to keep it for myself. I write a birthday message on the back and drop it in the bag. Landon said he'd be at home the whole day and wanted to be by himself. I respect that. I'd have done the same thing a few years ago, but as I get older the more I think I should celebrate making it to another year. Nonetheless, I ask him one more time, in case he changes his mind.

Are you sure you don't want to go out? We can have coffee later or a drink.

Yeah, I'm happy chilling in bed. I don't really want to see anyone.

Alright. I have something for you. I'll leave it at the foot of your stairs. Happy birthday.

Wow, thanks.

I walk over to his apartment and leave the yellow and white Loft bag at the bottom of the building's steps. To some extent I feel humiliated by all this bending over backwards, but more than that I'm hurt not to see him. It's a pity because it's a wonderful coincidence for me to be here. What were the chances? I think that's worth drinking to. Or at the very least, he could've peeked out or waved or smiled. Some sort of acknowledgement would've been nice. Before I walk away, still holding out hope to get a glimpse of him, I look up to his apartment for as long as I can and for as long as my pride lets me, but there is no sign of him.

I made plans to have lunch with Sebastian, and now

maybe even spend the whole afternoon with him, if he's free. He's curious to see Kagurazaka, a fascinating district I had told him about. It's considered to be Tokyo's French and Italian neighbourhood, not that he's looking for European cuisine. 'I want to eat Japanese food as much as I can,' he said. 'We don't have many Japanese restaurants in Mainz.' It's one of those contradictions in that he'd happily eat Japanese food but without the desire to go to Japan.

I'm eager to go back to Kagurazaka as I'm tormented by my failure to find the elusive New Zealand café. Through research, I'd learned that this coffee spot has one of the best flat whites. Finding it proved to be more difficult than I anticipated as I was working from a translation, and underlying that was the pride and insistence on finding it myself. Who knows, in our wanderings Sebastian and I may stumble upon it. I tell Sebastian on the phone to 'Take the A3 exit at Iidabashi', feeling much more confident – authoritative even – giving instructions. 'I'll meet you outside in front of Becker's.'

'Ha ha,' he said. 'You chose a German pub?'

'I know. We're not going there. Anyway, it's at the intersection of Mejiro and Sotobori, should you get confused.'

'Sure,' he said. Germans, at least the few I know, for some weird reason, seem to have taken to saying 'sure' for most things, in the same way some of my French friends like saying 'et cetera, et cetera' even though I don't know any native English speaker who uses it in everyday speech. I take the train and get there without a hitch. Moments later, another miracle. We find each other in front of Becker's.

'Hi!' Sebastian is exceptionally happy today. We walk along a major highway then turn onto an uphill street called Kagurazaka-dori. We're back to charming narrow roads, and Kagurazaka doesn't disappoint. It's a popular shopping district, moderately busy with motor and human traffic, packed with shops next to each other. One can find porcelain bowls and teapots, kimonos and electronics (of course) in between ramen and izakaya restaurants.

'Where are the European restaurants?'

'They're all in the alleys.'

At the top of the slope, before the street levels out, I see the unprepossessing sushi restaurant I call Sushi-Go-Round because those are the only words I can understand in its signage. There's nothing fancy about the place. We sit in the bar wrapped around the open kitchen, and as the name suggests, a conveyor belt tracks the entire length of the bar where little plates of sushi go by.

Sebastian's eyes light up and he immediately goes for a couple of them. Meanwhile, I look at the menu and order from the chef, an elderly man with a headband. I go for fish that isn't so common and is expensive in New York – varieties of mackerel like aji and sawara, marinated using heritage recipes. Oily fish like these can be too hardcore for some, but to be perfectly honest, when they're fresh, they're just as palatable as salmon or tuna. Sayumi was right when she recommended avoiding the hellish tourist trap, Tsukiji fish market, for incredible sushi. Good fish is everywhere, and Sushi-Go-Round has no shortage of it.

Sebastian has a healthy appetite and tends to keep conversation to a minimum while he eats, which is fine by me. He's lost quite a few pounds since the night I met him squirting burger juice on the hallowed walls of Pianos. He was never big, merely muscular back then. I suspect that the weight loss, which has now revealed a dramatic neck, has got to do with the lover.

'How do you find out about these places?' Sebastian asks at the end of his meal.

'I was fascinated to learn Tokyo has a French Quarter. But also, the last time I was here I was looking for a particular café, and I just couldn't find it.'

'Was it a French café?'

'New Zealand, actually. It's a coffee shop reputed to have the best flat white. We don't really have good flat whites in New York, if you can find them at all. But it seems here in Tokyo they've taken a liking to Australian and New Zealand coffee. I've never been to either of those countries so I'm eager to try them here.'

'And they say it's round here somewhere?'

'Okay, this was translated from somewhere, so we don't know how accurate it is. It says it's off Kagurazaka-dori. So, it's not on this street.'

'Wait, Kagurazaka-dori is different from Kagurazaka?'

'Yes, Kagurazaka is the neighbourhood. Kagurazaka-dori is this street.'

'Okay.'

'There's a T-junction here and on its corner is a Family Mart.'

'We walked by one.'

'Believe me I've been up and down that alley a hundred times. There are three Family Marts. The first isn't on a corner.'

'Sure.'

'The second is the one we saw and it's on a T-junction, but like I said I've searched high and low. There's a third one further up, but it's on a regular intersection. I've searched that area as well. And nothing.'

'Do you want to try looking for it after we've finished here?'

'I don't want to drag you all over the place. We'll walk around. I'll keep an eye open for it. If we find it, we find it.'

He looks at me more keenly. 'Your job is beginning to interest me.'

'Ha!'

'Let's ask for the bill. But I need to use the restroom. I hope it's not a squat toilet,' he says with a nervous laugh.

'Where does one even face?' I say agreeably.

'I suppose you face the hood because it shields the pee.' We share a hearty laugh.

When Sebastian comes back from the toilet, he says, 'It *was* a squat one.'

'I didn't want to scare you.'

'So, you knew!'

I laugh at him.

'Do you have them in the Philippines?'

'I've never seen them there. But let me tell you this. My father took me to his hometown in the countryside on one of the islands. We stayed in this house; I think it was his relatives'. It was more of a hut, really. So, I had to use the toilet, and – surprise! There was a ceramic bowl the size of a teacup sort of recessed in the ground. It was basically a hole in the ground. It was so small you had to have really precise aim. I've never seen anything like it. I was very young, and it scarred me for life.'

Sebastian giggles. We pay for our meal and head back out onto the streets. I take him to random back-alleys where we let ourselves get lost. There, along the tight, cobblestone pathways, we find the French restaurants, tucked between wooden houses with bamboo shades rolled down in front of their windows. It feels like the set of a samurai movie but then we stumble on crêpe restaurants with names like Fleur Bisous. It's strange, but it works. It's so charming I can't imagine it working the other way around. Imagine, say, wandering through Saint-Céneri-le-Gérei then coming across a Sushi-Go-Round. I don't see it the same way mainly because the Japanese can make great crêpes in Tokyo alleys, but raw fish would be grim in a medieval French village.

'I think I want something sweet,' Sebastian says.

We go downhill on Kagurazaka-dori, and across the highway, by the canal, is the aptly named Canal Café. I've been here before, sweating profusely under a flimsy umbrella, the sun beating down with an intent to melt it. From the sidewalk, we take the stairs down to the boardwalk on the banks of the canal. This time, long branches of blossom from the sakura on the sidewalk above cascade down over the trellis where we sit underneath. Boats are docked along the railings, and some are going out for a picturesque ride. On the other side of the canal, we see trains whizzing past behind an array of cherry trees.

'Well, this is another good one,' he says.

'It's nice, isn't it? But it's not really a find. As you can see, this is quite popular.'

'Sure, but I would never have found out about this place.'

I'd put myself in excellent standing with Sebastian when

I took him to a café a few feet from under the Manhattan Bridge, a gem of a hideaway on a decrepit block on the fringe of Chinatown. It had a collection of antique and vintage chairs to sit on, and in the summertime little flower-pots around its tiny window that would always be open. Every day they placed a child's wooden chair just outside of it, and thus the café was called Little Chair. The table by the window had a view of the bridge and the baseball park, and beyond it, the East River. They had great coffee made by long-haired Supreme hipsters who frequented the skateboard park nearby.

'We always look forward to your discoveries,' Sebastian says. 'We want to go back to Little Chair.'

'Unfortunately, Little Chair closed.'

'No! That's so sad. We loved it there.'

'When you say "we". . .'

❧

When I met Sebastian, he had been with his partner, Matthias, for close to twenty years. (Every now and then I have to remind myself that Sebastian is gay, and whenever I do it's a revelation. I think of him as straight, oddly enough.) One afternoon at Frankfurt Airport, after disembarking from a flight, he clapped eyes on Christian, a tall Australian-Asian super-hybrid who had just emerged from customs as if it were backstage of a runway show. Meanwhile, Sebastian in his uniform and black spinner carry-on luggage must have been a sight to behold. The double-take led to a conversation, and within minutes Sebastian was driving Christian to his hotel near Grünebergpark.

The attraction was mutual and undeniable, but Sebastian had to get home to Mainz, an hour away. The following day, Christian went to Mainz and had drinks with him, and by the end of the night they had decided to take things further. Sebastian drove him back to Frankfurt and spent the night there.

Sebastian met Christian twice more at his hotel in Frankfurt. That was when he suspected this was different. Sebastian and Matthias have an open relationship as well, and they follow the cardinal rule of open relationships: never fall in love. On the day Christian left Frankfurt, Sebastian drove him to the airport and used his special access and connections to send Christian to the furthest gate possible. At the very last barrier, where Sebastian could no longer go through to accompany him, it was clear that Sebastian had violated the most sacred rule. It was an emotional farewell. They promised to stay in touch, and Sebastian was inconsolable all the way back to Mainz.

Since then, not a day has passed that they don't communicate with each other. Christian lives in Singapore, and because of his 'neither' looks, he signed with an agency that gave him many assignments modelling for skin-whitening products in Asia and the Middle East. Sebastian did not have the seniority to change his route just yet, but by some stroke of luck, an opportunity opened up in the Frankfurt–Singapore route. Now I understood why I no longer saw him. One of Christian's more fortuitous assignments, however, was a gig in New York.

Sebastian got in touch with me one summer's day and said, *If you're in town, we'd like to get together. Maybe Little Chair again?* I was still unaware of the love affair at the time, so by 'we' I assumed it would be Sebastian and Matthias. Imagine my surprise when he walked into Little Chair that afternoon with Christian. We ordered coffee, and judging by Sebastian's attentiveness, I was beginning to suspect something was going on. We took the table by the window with the heat and brightness of a dazzling New York summer's day.

'This is really nice,' Christian said.

Sebastian looked at him and nodded, in the way lovers communicated with each other without the use of words. For the two seconds they looked at each other – just a momentary glimpse, and with an almost indiscernible smile at the corners of their lips – I knew. I could also tell they honestly loved the café for the very same reasons I did. It was a quiet, charmingly gritty nook somewhere in the big city, a spot few people knew about. And considering their situation, the feeling of surreptitiousness would've been amplified.

As far as I could tell over a cup of coffee, Christian seemed like a nice, level-headed guy with a disarming smile. He's in his early thirties and well aware that modelling isn't forever so he's transitioning into becoming a swimming coach and starting his own school. They were up for a stroll so when we were done, we went down to the FDR Drive and took the pathway along the East River. We walked up round the bend until we reached the East River Park. By the time we made it under the Williamsburg Bridge, I could tell that Christian was very much in love with Sebastian. We sat on a bench and watched tugboats go past the old Domino Sugar factory directly across the river. They're great together, although

I must say being with two tall, stunning creatures, a pilot and a model at that, is a considerable blow to one's self-esteem.

Sebastian would later tell me the whole story. I had wondered if he had split up with Matthias, but I was glad to learn he had not. That made the situation more complex, however. I'd noticed a huge difference in Sebastian since meeting Christian. Apart from the weight loss, he occasionally sent me photos of them on their trysts, and they both looked so happy. Genuinely happy. Seeing them together, they possessed an inexplicable joy and I couldn't fathom why they shouldn't be together. I suppose to keep this joy one doesn't necessarily have to give up everything one has.

*

'I guess by "we" I would mean Christian. We're *fagabond* lovers.'

'Listen to you,' I tease, although I'm not sure if the 'fag' is a pun. 'How long has it been? Two years?'

'Almost,' he says.

'Do you think Matthias knows?'

'He knows I see other people like he does. But he doesn't know I see one exclusively.'

'Do you feel guilty?'

'At first, I did not, but when I realised that I had feelings for Christian, then I felt guilty. Then after seeing him over and over, I'm just happy.'

'Have you thought of being together, just the two of you?'

'Sure. But I guess it would have worked twenty years ago. I don't think it would now.'

'Forty is still pretty young, don't you think? It's not like you're eighty-five looking back at the life you've wasted.'

'I know, but Matthias and I have been together for so long. My family has become his family and vice versa. How do you undo that? Imagine you and Gabriel. You have created a life together. It's your own world. Sometimes it's hard to see this, but it's there. Then you meet someone nice, for example. Nice enough to see many times. Then you start to see it's not easy to just leave all that behind.'

'No, especially if you still love each other in spite of all the circumstances.'

'Exactly. You love him through the years. I still love Matthias. It's not perfect, what we have. No couple is perfect. So it would have to be really, really bad for me. And it's not practical at all. Let's say Christian moved to Mainz: what would he do? He'd have to learn German for one thing. If you move here, for example, you have to learn the language. You have to learn all these squiggly things. I don't see it working, especially now he's started the swimming school.'

'What if, let's say, you find yourself happier with Christian? In your pictures you really look very, very happy. Wouldn't you come to regret that you didn't decide to be with him completely?'

'I remember something you said that time when Gabriel had an affair. You found out that he said he would regret it if he did not see the other guy again.'

'Strangely, I understood that.'

'I'm sure that made him happy the way I'm happy seeing Christian now. But I'm not leaving Matthias. And Gabriel did not leave you. Happiness is not the only consideration.'

Is that right? Do we not place happiness at the top of the list? Do we surrender to the life we've been living for the last five, ten, twenty years? Do we not give ourselves the chance for anything else? Or is it that, perhaps, the longing, the highs, and everything that makes for an epic love story will not, in the long run, live up to what it promises to be? Without the highs, there will be no lows, and maybe what's better and healthier, not just in love but in all of life, is the sustained, the stable, the secure – the settledness. There it is once again. Settledness. That I've heard it from Landon is the irony of it all.

Our order arrives, which abruptly lightens the mood. Upon my recommendation, Sebastian ordered a panna cotta made of kwanzan, a type of East Asian cherry. I'm having a selection of macarons in different flavours, which includes the best and most unusual I've ever had: yamamomo framboise. We both have coffee with the sweets, and after we finish everything, we hang around a little bit longer until they turn on the heat lamps. We enjoy the view, the trees, the boats, the canal, and it's hard not to be romantic, to take it all in, and everything else life throws at you.

'It's so special here,' Sebastian says. 'Christian would love it here.'

'It's too bad he couldn't come.'

'He wanted to, but he's very busy with the school. I'm going to Singapore for the first session on Sunday. Lots of kids.'

'It's fascinating. How do you deal with it? You have two lives.'

'The heart has four chambers, plus one more: the invisible one, where we find ourselves sometimes.'

I look at him in astonishment. I had no idea he's capable of such profundity. 'Sebastian. How did you come up with that?'

'Maybe it's all the flying and staring out into the sky!'

It's a little freaky when you meet someone and it feels like it's meant to be. It doesn't happen often for me or maybe I'm just not in tune with such things. Keeping a few coffee shops to myself is one thing, but Landon is another. Talking to Sebastian is almost like looking at a wise mirror that talks back. I've gleaned a great deal without having to reveal as much. It's incredible how parallel, in certain ways, our lives seem to be. Sebastian once dared use the word 'chemistry' to describe our friendship, so it's only fair that I get my own back this time.

'You know what?'

'What?'

'Us meeting here,' I say.

'What about it?'

'It's like destiny.'

Chapter Eleven

S ayumi wonders if I would be up for having ramen for dinner. I tell her that I would love to, but I'm in Kagurazaka with a friend who doesn't have dinner plans.

'Bring your friend,' she says.

She wants to take us to a restaurant from Tadami's college days in Aoyama Gakuin, a few minutes' walk from the famous crossing in Shibuya. We'll meet in front of the memorial for Hachiko, the legendary, beloved dog, which is the easiest and most recognisable landmark for us, never mind that it's at the heart of the crossing. It's quite funny to meet in front of a dog's statue, but then again, I'd met friends in front of Paddington Bear in London – and Paddington is fiction.

Sebastian is immediately excited upon learning where we're going.

'I've not been to the crossing yet,' he tells me.

Sebastian and I kill some time around the canal, crossing the bridge to the other side and exploring the neighbourhood, before taking the train to Shibuya. Sayumi is already there when we arrive. I introduce her to Sebastian.

'Sebastian has never crossed this,' I tell her.

Sayumi is appalled. 'What? We do this now!'

I don't think we really need to cross it, but what's a better way to break the ice? Hachiko stands in a plaza that's one of the corners of the famous crossing – commonly referred to as the scramble – where three of the wide pedestrian lanes come to a point. The scramble is roughly a hexagon, the sides being the pedestrian lanes, with one big lane cutting through the middle.

We're just at the top of rush hour, and huge crowds are building up at the corners. Right before the light changes, when the waiting crowd peaks, it looks like there's a revolution going on. Thank god the Japanese are very much into order, otherwise things could easily go wrong. Sayumi takes us towards the middle lane, which is the busiest and leads to a massive bookstore called Tsutaya.

The green man lights up. We begin crossing with hordes of people while dodging further hordes coming towards us, some on bicycles, some dragging spinner luggage of all sizes. Because all motor traffic is halted, pedestrians aren't bound to stay on the painted stripes and they go in all different directions. I wonder how we'll ever get past them, but incredibly, we make it halfway through. Tall buildings with LED lights blinking and flashing like fireworks make us feel like we're in the middle of the Milky Way. Amid everything, an insanely happy tune that sounds like music for a trippy children's show plays from somewhere. 'Bo beep beep, bo beep beep,' the music goes. We have no choice but to be ecstatic, and this is when it truly looks and feels like a scramble. It seems we might lose each other because there are so many people, busy and in a hurry, but there's also a great number of tourists, including Sebastian and me, who are simply in awe of the scale of something so common in life – crossing the street. When did something so mundane become such an incredible experience? Look at all these lives coming together. 'We're all just little white balls in a huge cosmological ping pong match,' the poet Toby Thompson once said, and at this exact moment, it couldn't be truer.

The green man starts to strobe, but we're still far from the other side. Sayumi makes some high-pitched noises and picks up her pace. Many others, perhaps having started late on their crossing journey, make a run for it. In full panic, Sebastian screams something in German that I cannot understand. 'Be island dish! Be island dish!' Half running, we just about make it to the other side when the roads are again taken over by vehicles.

We laugh insanely as if we've just survived bungee jumping or skydiving. At some point, Sayumi had taken out her phone to take a video of us. She shows us what she's taken, and we all notice that no one blocked her shot. Everyone dodged or ducked and stayed out of the way, and most extraordinary of all, despite the madness, not once was I jostled. It was the Japanese at their very best: polite and deeply reverent of personal space. After we collect ourselves, we walk away from the scramble as the number of people waiting to cross swells once more.

Sayumi leads the way to the ramen restaurant. It's a short walk to a low brick building in a leafy, slightly commercial area, but a lot quieter than where we'd just been. We approach what looks like the back entrance, by a giant, red accordion lantern emblazoned with large, black Japanese characters.

Like the ramen restaurant I went to on my first night, we order through a machine outside that ejects little stubs. It's one of those places where you need someone local to advise you on what to order, otherwise you may get a fish head or some other unexpected delicacy. Sayumi operates the machine for us, inserting an inordinate number of coins as the twenty or so buttons start flashing urgent green, similar to the strobing walk-signs of the scramble. Each button is labelled in Japanese. Some are in red, which I imagine would be spicy, and others green, which a vegetarian might hope does not contain whale or some other critically endangered species.

After we get our stubs, we go through a short passageway that cuts through the kitchen, ending in a cosy, wood-panelled dining area. In fact, everything in the restaurant is shiny wood. You would almost expect to smell varnish. A server seats us at a corner table and we hand him our stubs. The beauty of ramen is that it's served expeditiously. There's a huge vat of broth bubbling away somewhere, and the noodles cook for less than a minute. The chef assembles the bowl and it's ready to be served.

Sayumi and Sebastian hit it off, although I can't imagine them not doing so. It's too bad Tadami couldn't join us on account of his jujutsu match. It would have been very interesting to see them all interact with each other. I let Sayumi and Sebastian bond, talking about their experiences in New York. He tells her how we met at Pianos and about the squirting hamburger. Sebastian loves that story as much as I do. At some point in their conversation I overhear him ask Sayumi where he can shop for men's 'cloths'.

I get a moment to look at my phone, and that's when

I see that I've received an email from my immigration lawyer. My heart pounds. Has the petition come through? It can't be. It would be too easy. It cannot be good news. I get a feeling that something has gone wrong because in my experience dealing with the matter has never been plain sailing. Whatever it may be exactly, I can't open it right now. I put my phone away and try to forget it.

It's never fun when something so critical preoccupies the mind, but I succeed in enjoying the meal and the company. After we finish, we amble back to Hachiko at Shibuya station. We stand there at the plaza, three wide pedestrian lanes fanning out. Sebastian is flying out tomorrow for Singapore to go on with his journey. Sayumi goes back to Tennozu Isle, and it's unlikely I'll see her again before I leave. One day I'll come back to see her. If you could award Michelin stars to a person, I'd give her three. She is worth making a special journey for.

I go back to Shimokitazawa for now, with trepidation of what's beyond. We're all on a crossroads. Our journeys are much wider and more immense than the destination, which, come to think of it, can sometimes be variable. Where do we go? Should we go back to the familiar? Should we take a different course? We don't cross the scramble again. This time we descend beneath the ground to take different trains, but nonetheless we make the farewell this incredible coincidence deserves.

On the train I get the solitude to read the email. It's business hours now in New York so the sooner I reply, the clearer the picture, the closer I am to a resolution. I have enough courage now to open it. It's what I expected.

I received a hold notice regarding your petition for a work visa. It doesn't specify what is holding it up, but it is likely that they are looking for additional supporting documents. I will let you know as soon as possible what we need to come up with when they send the request. At the moment it is difficult to estimate how long this process will take. I am sorry to say that it is unlikely you will make it to your appointment at the embassy next week. At this point I think it is best that you reschedule.

Through the years I'd gotten better at reacting to this situation. This, or something similar, has happened many times before. Though I know now there's no point in panicking, it gets more frustrating each time. There's only so much one can struggle, and the more important question is, how long can I sustain it? How many times and for how much longer will I be doing this?

Blue Liberica had given me three weeks off. If everything had gone according to plan, I'd have my appointment at the Manila embassy next week, get my passport back after five days, with plenty of time before flying back to New York. Now I have to move the appointment, which would likely be in a month's time. That also means moving the return flight. With the new schedule, will I get the approval in time? There's no way of knowing. This could take months. My life is on hold.

Thoughts of settling back in Manila always cross my mind whenever this happens, but the longer I live in New York, the harder it is to imagine. People who find themselves in a similar situation often argue with the authorities, 'But what about my life?' It's true. My life is there, but it's not an argument to be made at the embassy. Consuls care about documents, not drama. I don't necessarily want to be an American, but I am a New Yorker. If only there was a visa for New York. Maybe that would be easier.

Outside of Shimokitazawa station I write my reply. *I'll send whatever is needed as soon as I can.*

My feet are taking me in the direction of Garden View, but I don't feel like going home. I can't go to sleep just yet. I'm tired, but I need to be exhausted. I need to run myself into the ground so when I go to bed there won't be a second spared to worry about anything. I don't look for alcohol per se, but a drink might do me good. Instead of going left I go in the opposite direction, towards the alleys of shops and restaurants. Some of them are about to close, but the streets are still fairly busy. I check out bars on upper floors in the hope I'll discover a tranquil spot, but right when I think it might be, it turns out it's a smoking bar. Sayumi's words come to mind. 'Japanese people smoke a lot.'

I don't mind looking for other places. I walk further down familiar side streets, until I finally see the flower shop Landon told me about. It's quite dim, but from the street I can make out no more than ten people inside. Surely they can't be buying flowers at this time of night?

I walk in inquisitively, and true enough, a bartender is serving drinks. He smiles at me and gestures to an empty seat at the bar. The buckets of flowers have been moved to one side by the windows, and the effect is just lovely. He hands me the menu, the size of a greeting card. They don't have a very wide selection of drinks, only the classics. I ask the bartender, a middle-aged man, if he can make me a French 75 with cognac.

'You like a real cocktail!'

His enthusiasm is a good sign. 'Can you do it?'

'I have no champagne. Prosecco okay?'

'That's perfect.'

'Where are you from?'

'I live in New York.'

'Ah!' He's visibly enlivened. 'I go there a lot. I live in Queens, and I take R train.' It takes me a moment to understand that he's talking about the past, and I smile. He's learned to speak English strictly in the present tense, a phenomenon that's not exactly new to me. I've met a few New Yorkers who speak this way, as if they only live in the present like animals in the wild – which is somewhat unsurprising for the jungle that is New York. He had often travelled there in the not-so-distant past to visit his wife who used to work in Manhattan. He recalls fond memories and reminisces about his routines. 'I don't like it,' he adds with a dreamy, faraway look.

The discrepancy between his words and his nostalgia perplexes me. Is it possible that he may not have liked it, but misses it? He quickly changes the topic and tells me Dan is performing. He gives me this information as if I ought to know who Dan is. *You know, Dan. Oh yeah, yeah, yeah. Dan. Of course. Who else?* But then I think, whoever Dan may be, as long as I have my drink, I'll be fine.

A few minutes later a man in a suit and a bowler hat slowly worms his way to the end of the small space, which is extra-challenging for him on account of the accordion strapped across his body. This must be Dan. He gets in position, and everyone settles down. He says a few things in Japanese, which makes everybody laugh, and I smile because what does one do in such situations? He casts his eyes down for a moment, and his right hand begins to fiddle with the keyboard while his left presses the ivory buttons. The bellows expand and the distinct sound of the instrument fills the tiny room. The scent of flowers all around, the heady cocktail and Dan's music altogether challenge my presence here. I am transported, lost. Where am I? Am I in the old town of Mainz or on the steps of the Sacré-Coeur?

Dan ends his set after a couple more tunes, and long after the applause has ended, I'm still in a daze. The bartender tells me the shop is closing soon, so I pay up before I finish my drink, which has been excellent. *Have I had two or three?* I should be able to tell by the amount on the bill. It's in the thousands, and I'm glad to realise it's in yen. Be that as it may, I've lost my ability to convert currencies, so I simply pay what the bill tells me. I say goodbye to the bartender and he says, 'Goodbye, New Yorker!' I shake his hand hoping that 'New Yorker' is a foreshadowing, not a jinx.

Outside, I zip my jacket tightly to my neck. The neighbourhood is still and silent. The sadness hits me. I'm neither in Mainz nor in Montmartre, but would I want to be there? I'm in Shimokitazawa. I'm in Tokyo at the peak of the cherry blossom. This is the escape. One can't escape from the escape. The next few months may be uncertain, but for now, I know where to go. I know that the side street from the flower bar will cut through the neighbourhood and take me closer to my street. I walk away from the antique shops and little restaurants whose metal shutters are now rolled down. I've come to realise that without the people and their energy, the distinct quirkiness hidden from view, everything is basically tatty, but charming. They do tatty very well here in this city.

The alley gets narrower and quieter the further I go. Normally I'd be vigilant for an assailant, but there's nothing to worry about in Tokyo. There's no crime in Japan, Sayumi assured me. I can walk insouciantly through dark sections of the alley. I make it to a block of mostly homes save for a three-storey building halfway down. I walk slower to examine the small window of what appears to be a bar or a restaurant on the first floor. On the windowsill are sake bottles with their labels facing outward – clearly an invitation. The lights are on and from the street it looks inviting. Is it as enchanting as the flower bar? Assessing if they're still open, I hear a hubbub of laughter from a group of young men and women, maybe five or six of them, coming down the spiral staircase in front of the building.

When they make it down to the street, I realise that the cacophony is in English. I glance casually at them, and before I look away, I notice the boy behind everyone else. The silhouette. There's no mistaking it. He steps into better light, just enough for me to make out the black bomber jacket, open to reveal the denim jacket underneath. I don't know anyone else who layers this way. The cacophony is clearly a festive ruckus, a celebration of sorts, and I understand. *But you said. . .*

Landon sees me looking at him, his blue eyes beaming through the tenebrous street, and with a faint smile, his face obscured by a shadow like the photograph I took, he nods to me unashamedly. One nod, one bob of the head. I struggle to react, to deal with the treachery he so casually demonstrates. Reflexively I return the smile, as faint and as minuscule, a quick defensive reaction to save face, to save my pride, like I don't care, like it doesn't hurt. One of them shouts 'Come on!' and he's swept away by his happy and boisterous friends, to whom I seem to be invisible, down another alley. Quicker than a minute they've all disappeared and the sudden disturbance is gone as swiftly as it came. What feels real, however, is that I'm again an outsider looking in. I never did own a clear plastic umbrella; I'm not one of them. I don't belong in their world. I seem to have been paralysed on the street, and when I remember I was actually on the way to somewhere, I start moving again, stupefied, one foot in front of the other down the alleyway, in and out of the shadows and occasional light.

Chapter Twelve

'There's a pair of jeans that I'm thinking of getting, and I'd like to get your opinion,' Landon says over the phone. There's no mention of what happened last night nor a touch of guilt or remorse in his voice. It makes me feel like I'm being oversensitive. Am I making too much out of it? Am I mistaken in feeling wronged when he said he'd not wanted to see *anyone* and did the opposite? The invalidation of my feelings is infuriating.

I could say something about it, but I'm feeble. I can't even bring it up. There's something much more powerful in me, drawing me to pull out all the stops to please him. I'm won over by the flattery of his request. My opinion matters to him. I should be so lucky. To what do I owe this honour? To be considered an arbiter of style? Now this truly feels like a game. I'm aggravated I'm playing along, but I can't stop myself. I just want to see him, so I'll suffer the full indignity of it. After sending a few emails to my lawyer, I go to him like yesterday.

I get to Landon's apartment much earlier than usual. I'm surprised he's up, but there he is, carrying on as before. We sit face to face at the kitchen table and he pours me coffee, smirking in a superior manner as if nothing has

happened. How ironic that acting like this only empha-
sises the fact something actually has.

'What's going on?' he asks in that slightly accusing
manner. It makes me nervous even though there is absolutely nothing to be nervous about. I'm not the one who
lied, and yet why am I the one on edge? Suddenly I'm
faced with the truth that I don't really have the pluck to
stand up for myself. 'You said you were writing an email
to your lawyer.'

'Oh.' I'm relieved he's not talking about last night. I shy
away from any sign of confrontation. 'Yeah. Not very
good news. I had a fitful sleep waiting for emails.'

'Why's that?'

I tell him about the whole situation. I tell him that I've
moved my appointment at the embassy, and the soonest I
could get is, as predicted, five weeks from yesterday. I've
sent an email to my airline to move my return, and I've yet
to hear back from them. I would've called, but my phone
doesn't make international calls. I've also been in touch
with work. They say I have enough work banked in for at
least three more weeks, for which I will still get paid. After
that, we'll have to reassess how to go from there. That I
only have a few sets of clothes and two pairs of shoes is the
least of my worries – for now. If at the conclusion of this
is a life back in Manila, then I'd have to start the process of
repatriating all my belongings.

'You'll be fine,' is all I hear from him. I had the impres-
sion that he was concerned, or at the very least interested,
to hear all about it, so I did my best to convey the com-
plexity and gravity of the situation. Now all I get is 'you'll
be fine'. Could he be more dismissive? His indifference

amazes me, considering he understood his brother's girl-friend's situation, and he *himself* is a foreign worker. Perhaps, at the end of the day, he is British, and all his life he's been able to wield that powerful passport, never facing any difficulties emigrating, much less travelling. It would therefore be easy to be dismissive of people's tra-vails when you've never really experienced anything like it yourself.

It riles me enough to bring up last night. 'What about you? What did you do last night?' I had intended to say it much more confrontationally than it sounded, but at least I managed to speak up.

'Had drinks with some friends,' he says offhandedly. 'I was being a total expat.'

I don't know what he means by that, and I don't bother to ask. I simply want to get a rise out of him, but he really is unbothered by it. I should have pushed more, but instead I have given him a free pass. I put on a small smile to keep myself from appearing hurt. 'Sounds fun,' I say, hoping it appears as empty as 'you'll be fine'. I'm not very good at this.

Landon rises to get something from the fridge. In the corner of my eye, I see the yellow and white Loft paper bag, empty, wrinkled and cast off to a corner near the sink next to a garbage bag, destined for the inevitable disposal. It's interesting that without its original contents, the bag, wide open and valiantly upright from what remains of its stiffness, has quickly lost its dignity despite what's embla-zoned on it, and what it claims it's worth. 'Look, I'm a Loft bag! I have value!' This is exactly how I feel. I'm the Loft paper bag. I don't see the plates anywhere, so he must have stashed them where I can't see them. At least I hope he did.

Clearly, I don't mean anything to him. I imagine him yesterday, quickly off to get the bag at the foot of the stairs to mitigate the embarrassment. In his haste to rid himself of the plates he must've overlooked the postcard, which is still probably in the bag within the crumpled tissue paper. I loved that postcard, and wish I'd gotten at least one more if only I'd had the foresight. I wanted to keep it for myself but instead I gave it to him. I gave it to him because he meant something to me. 'To Landon,' I had inscribed on the back, 'the boy from England who moved to Tokyo, whom I met in New York, where I lived.' Now I feel like the biggest fool for writing mawkish billet-doux and trawling around town buying plates with money I could have kept for my possible impending unemployment.

Just when I feel most vanquished, when I concede everything is futile, I glance up at the window above us. Propped up on the sill next to the three candles in ascending height: the postcard. My belligerence is instantly put to rest.

'I have some yoghurt,' he says, rifling in the fridge. 'Weren't you looking for some?' Indeed, I have been looking for yoghurt, but all the ones I've seen are so runny. I must have mistaken something else for yoghurt, or yoghurt really is runny in Japan. 'Do you want some now? You can take this with you. It's yours.'

'Thanks.'

'You know, the other night, I got sexually harassed by two high school girls. Sometimes I get treated as this exotic object,' he says without a hint of indignation. In fact, it turns him on. He slides the tips of his fingers from my shoulders down to my elbow. The sensation immobilises me. What's wrong with me? A minute ago, I was furious, and now I am thrilled with his advances and hoping for more. He kisses my neck very tenderly and grabs my arm a tad too forcefully to take me to the bed. I no longer have control of myself – if I ever had any. He straddles me, and in a change of pace, he takes it slow, pulling his T-shirt over his head. He looks at me with puppy eyes then slides his shorts off. My feelings for his glorious body haven't changed. I admire his nakedness and majestic arousal. He's so stiff it slaps against his abdomen with a thud. He pins me down, holding my wrists above my head. He kisses me hungrily. His tongue whirls in my mouth like how I wish he'd explore my emotions. Just like the last time we had sex, when I barely kept up with him, his intensity is through the roof.

He gets me naked as quickly as if it were one of those tricks when the tablecloth gets pulled out from under without disturbing the dinnerware on it. He exhales through his mouth like it's a proud accomplishment. I try my best to reciprocate the lechery, to be as thirsty as he is. I writhe under his hard, naked body on top of me, and on my bare skin I feel the unmistakable slippery wetness he leaks copiously. This is something that cannot be faked. He truly is into me and comes on way too strong even if I am attracted to him. Despite the frantic Sisyphean stroking, I won't pull this off like I did the last time. I'm too overwhelmed. I'm too preoccupied. Too many elements have come into the mix alongside what used to be just the simple ingredient that is carnal desire. He knows. He senses it.

'You're not hard,' he says in a soft voice.

'I'm sorry. We can try later?'

'It's okay. Don't fret over it.' He rolls over, and we lie next to each other closely.

'I have a few things on my mind.'

'Would you like to have a walk about?' he asks.

'That would be nice,' I say, although I would've preferred him to ask me what's on my mind, or to have commiserated with me over my uncertain future. I wish I were over the hurt from last night. I wish I had the ability to be sexual without the strings, because to me this is no longer a one-night stand that goes on indefinitely. But that's on me.

'We can grab a bite at Daisho.'

I have forgotten what Daisho is, and don't bother to ask. We get dressed and venture out. It has just rained, and the sun's rays through the moist air have that optimistic quality. Even the glistening ground evokes hope. A fresh start. Or perhaps it's my imagination and hopeless optimism.

We head in the direction of the big supermarket, and Daisho turns out to be the recommended sushi restaurant with kaisen dons for less than five American dollars. One cannot miss it. Its two signs are truly bigger than it is. Inside it's cosy and warm, and the wooden interior makes me feel like we're in a sauna. He knows I'll eat anything, so he orders for us. When the food comes, none of the dishes is a kaisen don. Instead, there's edamame, miso soup, sashimi in a beautifully presented bowl with crushed ice, and a big plate of egg, mackerel and octopus sushi. This feast will be more than five American dollars, that I can be sure of. Annoyingly, I enjoy the meal and the company, and he knows it.

'So, what's with these jeans?'

'I need to improve my wardrobe. I wish I didn't have such fashionable friends.'

'Oh, come on. You're okay. You shouldn't worry about that.'

'I just feel like I need to take it up a notch.'

The jeans shop isn't far from Daisho. It's a small storefront carrying a brand I've never heard of, and it doesn't seem to be something he would learn about through his own initiative. It's definitely something cool, something trendy – or even more short-lived, *trending* – that his fashionable peers have unintentionally pressured on him. He picks a few pairs on a shelf and a young saleswoman shows him to a cramped fitting room. He tries on a grey pair first, stepping out to show me, examining them in front of a full-length mirror. From the front they look fine, but he turns around and it's quite noticeable that the buttocks and upper thigh sag a bit. He notices the flaws, too, and goes back to try the next pair. It's a similar cut, but this time everything is snug, in fact a bit too snug for my taste. He goes on to try two more, and I conclude all of them are exceedingly tight; I can't imagine how anyone can disrobe without turning them inside out. I don't see the appeal of painted-on jeans on men. But since he's partial to them, the last pair would be the best, if he were to get any of them.

'What do you think?'

They do look good on him. They're dark and faded at the knees. His thighs are showcased beautifully, and from behind, his calves much more than the butt, which in effect makes the jeans unequivocally menswear. 'Still sexy with clothes on?' he had asked me that morning in New York. I had not even entertained the idea that one's sexiness can be reversed after putting clothes on, once you've seen what's underneath and liked it. To me, if I know how the person looks naked, he can wear a garbage bag and I'll still find him sexy.

'It's up to you,' is what I say.

He takes a serious look at the mirror, turning both ways. 'They're nearly but not quite,' he says. I check the price, and they're nearly but not quite three hundred dollars. In the end he doesn't take them.

After the jeans shop, he takes me to Village Vanguard, a huge store named after the New York jazz club. It's filled with snacks, stuffed toys, knickknacks and novelties. We try on nerdy glasses with fake eyes and laugh at each other. I feel like we're in a montage of an old movie. The store has so much stuff that after a while my eyes start to get blurry from sensory overload. We leave and hit the alleys once more. He thinks I'll like old furniture, so we look at a few dusty shops that sell vintage furniture and kitchenware. We go inside several vintage clothing stores, one of which is called New York Joe Exchange. All these New York references amuse me, but the Japanese have such a strong sense of identity that it doesn't look and feel like they're aping New York.

Outside New York Joe, Landon tells me he needs to answer a message on his phone. I cross the street to give him a moment. I stand in front of a restaurant directly opposite the store. It's devoid of windows, except for an aquarium installed in its external wall. In it are six or seven fugu, each one about a foot and a half long, swimming calmly. Fugu are pufferfish, a culinary delicacy that contains a deadly poison, so chefs must be specially qualified to prepare them, or it could be fatal to the consumer. Mottled on the sides, their glowing white underbellies mesmerise me as they move to and fro.

Moments later I snap out of my reverie and turn around. He's still twiddling with his phone, standing on the same spot where I left him. But as always, you can rely on his uncanny awareness of me – he looks up from his phone as if I've called out his name. He looks fixedly at me; his eyes are so light in the sun. He's wearing the same combination of bomber jacket over denim jacket, dark jeans and Vans slip-ons. My eyes are drawn, for some reason, to the clear umbrella hanging off his left arm, and something inside tells me that I've got to talk to him.

He puts his phone away and we go onwards, wandering down the street. I'm not really sure who's leading who at this point until we walk by Café Use. The familiar Harley-Davidson is, as always, parked in front of it. We don't even look or say anything to each other. Without a word we go in and, being a Saturday, the café is the busiest I've seen it. Despite that, our preferred table at the back corner is unoccupied and we take our usual places, Landon by the wall with legs sideways. Anyone would think we've done this routine a million times, like we've compressed years of togetherness in such a short time.

A lady comes over to hand us the menu and leaves. He mumbles something about milk, but I don't catch it. I don't even know what I want. I can't even remember what I asked for when the server comes back to take our order. At this point, all I'm thinking is, *What do I say? How do I start?* It's been days since I stood under the cherry blossom by the river, overwhelmed by this urge to see him again despite having spent the day and the previous night together. With all that has happened since, whatever I have to say has grown deeper and more complex. It's so complex that sex isn't just sex. It's more than that. It's definitely more than that.

'About earlier. . . there's a lot going on right now, as you know. It's more than the visa thing. I really like you. I find you very attractive. But it's more complicated than that.'

I search for the words to go on, to say that since I met him and especially since spending all this time with him, my feelings for him have grown and become so powerful that they have left me in a state of flux. It seems so easy to articulate, but at that moment, face to face in Café Use, it's not as effortless to make sense of and find the right words.

'I'm into you,' he says before I can continue. 'I'm into you, but I always hit a ceiling of how much I like the person I'm sleeping with. Nobody's managed to break that ceiling for about four years now. Before that it wasn't too hard.'

I'm baffled by what he's just said. For a moment I think I've misheard him, but he did say it. I'm stunned. *Where did that come from?* He must think I'm attempting to put an end to this, which I'm not. I simply don't want him to think that I've stopped liking him just because I couldn't match his intensity in bed. I really do like him, and I don't want him to think otherwise. But it's as if I got there before him, so he goes on the offensive, bringing up this business about breaking ceilings.

I wasn't asking you to love me!

It becomes clear to me, and I'm very saddened to see,

that to him it *is* a game. In my heart I believed he was playing games, perhaps not initially, but eventually it had become one, and it's hard to admit that I'd been right. I've been so credulous, and still so credulous that instead of explaining what I've just said, I take the bait and allow him to steer the conversation his way.

'Have I hit this ceiling?' I ask.

'Just about,' he says. 'I guess I have some kind of sexual ADD. Concentration issues. I don't need variety. I need people to understand that sometimes I have my moments and sometimes I don't.'

I have my moments and sometimes I don't. Says the boy who leaks like a tapped maple tree. It's such a lie. Sexual ADD – what nonsense. Never heard of such a thing. If anyone should have it, it should be me.

Whatever it is you suffer from, I can be sure of one thing.

The server approaches bearing a tray. She places our cups on the table, which clink softly in their saucers, as if trembling in fear of what I'm about to say. She turns her back to us and walks away.

'You've never stayed long enough for anyone to notice you grind your teeth at night.' Landon stares blankly at me as if I've made some unremarkable comment on something we've seen on the street. How can that not have made any impact? No one, in the last four years of sleeping around, has ever told him about it because not one of those encounters had been deep, long and meaningful enough.

I mind my coffee to avoid catching his eye. I look around the café. I look everywhere but him. I study a high shelf above the doorway, close to the ceiling, holding a collection of antique Coleman lanterns, coffee grinders and roasters. I notice our table is a battered school desk and the booth dividers are old wood-framed windowpanes. Everything in the café seems to be salvaged from homes made a hundred years ago. Without looking at him I notice he has not touched his coffee, steaming forthrightly from the cup. How can I have forgotten? He has damned cat's tongue. He can't handle hot, but this time there's nothing remotely funny about it. He drinks his coffee unperturbed, almost with a total disregard or even a dismissal of me. We sit in interminable, expressionless silence, under severe shadows and at the mercy of Chet Baker, whose trumpet playing is undeniably mournful, but whose singing is a punch in the gut. I don't know how long I can stand it. I get up to use the restroom and take my time. When I come out, before I take my seat back in our booth, I see him through the ribbed glass divider, and his image is vertically split and scattered. He's cleaved into pieces as if he's several people in a vain attempt to be one individual. I can't make out his face, but he looks up and five blue eyes stare back at me.

I take my seat. 'I don't want to be patronising,' Landon says, 'but people who are into me find they get over me very quickly.'

Translation: 'You're not breaking up with me; I'm breaking up with you.'

It's so petty and incredibly annoying. He has deployed that mock modesty once again. It could just be his style – I'll never know. But in case it's real, an honest deficiency in self-esteem, I stop myself from saying something mean or snide because I care about him. 'You should stop doing this, you know. Selling yourself too short. You're worth more than you think.'

We ask for the bill and the server places a small wooden tray with a piece of paper on the table. We leave money and get up to leave. We walk by the bar and under the shelf of antique lanterns. He slides the front door open. We step out onto the street and stand next to the motorcycle.

'I don't want to leave it like this,' I tell him. He looks at me intensely in the way he has before, when I believed him, when I thought he wasn't playing games and spewing rubbish like ceilings and sexual ADD. I steady myself because, for some reason, I know I'll believe him. Whatever he says at this moment, I'll believe him.

'I can't imagine you leaving behind the life you've already made.'

And he wins. He wins not only because it's true, it's indisputable. Suppose it comes to that. Would I move here? Would I give up New York? Probably not. Perhaps the visa will decide. But I want the choice to stay or go to be my own. If it were decided for me, I'd never get over the fact that it wasn't my initiative. I should be glad it doesn't even come to that. It's nowhere near that. Harley-Davidson as our witness, the words I hear cut to the chase with such profound finality. *I can't imagine you leaving behind the life you've already made.*

I have nothing more to say. I don't know what to say. In silence we walk the short distance to the junction with the useless stoplight where we found ourselves just a few days ago. He crosses straight ahead back to his apartment, and though I know that going left, as he had told me, will lead me back to Garden View, I'm no less disoriented than the day he showed me the way.

Chapter Thirteen

I had arranged a call with my work colleague Deniece before she went out for her weekly Saturday singing engagements, which works perfectly since I'm still jet-lagged and up at ungodly hours. I explain to her the whole situation. 'So, I need to have the number of likes, comments and views tied to sales figures,' I tell her. 'And obviously a glowing review of my work, that I came up with the coffee shop challenge, that we've increased our followers, that sort of thing.'

'I know what you need,' she says. I can imagine her winking. Deniece reads and interprets our analytics, and such information has to come from a figure of authority within the company. As Blue Liberica's Senior Marketing Director, Deniece can sign documents with the company's letterhead and vouch for my work.

Before he signed off for the weekend, my lawyer had dutifully sent me a list of documents he needed to re-file my petition at the immigration bureau. 'It would be great if you could gather your best work and statistics that go with them. We need to show that what you post or write for your marketing campaigns yield results. Those will help.'

I've been content – at least on my personal accounts – that I'm not on an empty quest for likes and followers like many people on social media. And yet, to be able to stay in New York I'll be measured by exactly that. I look back at my college years in Manila when I was taking marketing, and never did I imagine there would be such a thing as social media. We went to the library to go on the World Wide Web, on massive beige computers with screens for everyone to see. We didn't spend all our waking hours on it, and now our life depends on it. Thankfully we can now indulge our guilty pleasures in the privacy of our own phones.

'I imagine the coffee shop challenge has been the most popular. It should have a good following. Sorry to bother you with all this.'

'That's okay,' Deniece says. 'I know about your hate-hate relationship with social media.'

She understands. A singer herself, she makes a living wage posting inane captions like 'Comment below and tell us what you think!' I hear her typing notes on her computer, and I picture her long artificial nails like a crab crawling sideways.

'Alright,' she says. 'I'll get these to you on Monday.'

'Thank you.'

'Good luck, darling. Let me know how it goes. Miss you deep,' she says.

I'd given Gabriel an update on the matter and he's very concerned, but not concerned enough to propose marriage. Knowing me well enough, he strikes the right balance between concern and confidence that everything will be ironed out eventually. I did receive a couple of marriage proposals, one from a straight female friend whom I've known for donkey's years. She had messaged me and said simply, 'We can get married.'

The other was from a former work colleague named Michael, who quit to become a full-time hairdresser. He had been wanting to get an update from me so I call him after I've wrapped up my phone call with Deniece.

'Hey, poopy,' he says. He likes calling me poopy, which is quite unusual for a bearded bear of a man.

Michael is a recovering alcoholic who has recently started drinking again. I wouldn't say he's relapsed, like he must have a drink the minute he wakes up, but he has a drink the minute he finishes work, which would be right about now. For the most part he's a nice gentle soul, but there's something slightly scary about him when he's tipsy, especially when he has shears in his hands.

'Hey, I was thinking about you, and I told myself, "You know what, I'd marry him." I'd marry you if you need it,' he says.

I can now definitely say Michael's drunk, but I also know that he means it. He's a good friend, but quite complicated, as complicated as the whole endeavour itself. It's something that should really only be considered as a last resort, when all else fails. The marriage process takes years and it's a huge commitment to fraudulence. I for one have trouble remembering where Michael's from and one needs to know these things, among a whole host of other pieces of personal information. I always confuse Albany with Buffalo, and I can only just remember it because of his favourite dish.

'Buffalo,' he'd correct me. 'Like Buffalo wings.'

'Thanks for the offer, really,' I say. 'If this doesn't go through, let's look into that.'

After I hang up from Michael, I get a moment to soak in Garden View. I open the window to let the light in and look at the tree that stands outside so reliably. My mind drifts off and I think of Landon. Why do I always think of him? I get a moment to myself and he's all I think about.

I receive a photo from Sebastian in Singapore. He's half submerged in a swimming pool with Christian, smiling with a handful of kids wearing swim caps and goggles. *First lessons*, he wrote. Christian's career transition has begun with Sebastian alongside him. How long Sebastian will be able to live his double life, I can only guess. Whichever way it goes, of course I wish him to be at his happiest. But how do you know that? How do you know where you're happiest?

New York seems like a world away and though I'd like to be back, I have one full day left in Tokyo. That's today. Tomorrow, I leave. My happiness here will be different from my happiness elsewhere. I understand that things have shifted between me and Landon. If our lives travelled in an orbit, the closest we come to each other has come to pass. We're now drifting apart, and in light of yesterday, whatever we have has ended.

If I had a shred of self-respect, I'd never speak to him again. All those things he came up with, sexual ADD, the ceiling – it's all nonsense. It's infuriating and irritating. It's unfortunate the way it has turned out, but I don't regret coming to Tokyo. And after everything this week has given me, the beauty all around and the joys that filled my heart, I would deeply, sorrowfully regret that I passed up the chance to see him. Not only do I have a day, but I'm also no more than ten minutes away. If I shed all pretences and pride, if I give in to that basic, innermost desire, in all honesty my happiest wish would be to see him for as long as I possibly could. And so however misguided or perverted this happiness may be, however full of contradiction, I try to get past the indignation and shame to ask for it.

'I only have a day left,' I tell him over the phone. 'Can we make the most of it?'

'Of course,' he says.

'I have a nine a.m. checkout tomorrow but my flight isn't until five. I was thinking I could spend the night so I don't have to be at the airport so early. I'll have all that time to spend with you.'

Part of me hopes he says no to save me from myself. Incredibly, he says, 'That's no problem.' Even more incredibly, he says, 'Why don't you come now? Though I do have a party to go to later in the afternoon, just to warn you.'

Yes, I know you're busy and elusive and mysterious and a fucking enigma.

'Why don't you let me know when you're back? I can come anytime. I don't mean to disrupt your day. As I said, I'll have all that time tomorrow, unless you're busy.'

'No, on Mondays my class is at six-thirty.' *Like last Monday. You finish at nine-thirty.* 'Come now.'

'Okay, but not right this minute,' I say. 'I have to pack. I'll come as soon as I finish.'

What kind of person have I become? A fool, that's what I am, but I can't help myself. I'm delighted to have the time with him and, despite my doubts, it feels like he's doing this out of enjoyment. I mean, if he never wants to see me again, he wouldn't have picked up my call. I pack my bags hastily and carefully go over the checkout instructions. I would hate to be blacklisted from this apartment. With my duffel bag hanging over my shoulder, I lock up Garden View and make my way to his apartment.

'Make yourself at home,' he says. I put my bags down in front of the shoji.

'I hope it's not too much of a hassle.'

'No worries.' There's something different in his manner and his tone. I try to make conversation, but he's deliberately aloof and taciturn. He doesn't look me in the eye. He keeps himself at a distance. I try to brush it off because he did ask me to come, and urgently at that. 'I hope you don't mind if I tidy up while you're here.'

'Of course not. If I can be of help. . .'

'It's alright. This tiny place won't take long.'

'I can't *not* do anything. How about the dishes?'

'Alright,' he concedes.

In a fit of zealousness, he vacuums with his rechargeable Dyson. He organises, albeit slipshod, some of his paperwork. He then goes into the bathroom and closes the door. I hear the water running, and then it sounds like he's losing a wrestling match with a gorilla inside. He comes out naked and wet. I hand him his towel.

'Don't close the door,' he says. 'Let it dry for a bit.'

I look over and the toilet seat, the lid, the shelves – even the mirror – are all dripping. It turns out he hosed it down with the hand-held shower and showered after. I may have been right about why these bathrooms are moulded plastic. He's dripping on the floor, and if there's something else I could've bought for his birthday it would've been a shower mat. He doesn't have one, and I suppose he uses his towel to dry his feet. That doesn't bode well for me because I know I'll be sharing it later.

After drying himself Landon puts on a clean pair of boxers. 'What do you think of this?' he asks, holding up a grey, long-sleeved, checkered shirt. It's the second time he's sought my fashion opinion. He must hold me in some regard.

'I've never seen you wear that,' I say, and I'm proud of replying obliquely to match his chilliness. He falls to his knees in front of the ironing board and gingerly irons the shirt. It pains me to see him awkwardly positioned like a grasshopper. 'You need a better ironing board.'

'Like what?'

'Maybe waist-high?' I shrug. He smiles to himself. I don't understand why it has to be legless, or maybe they're meant to be placed on a table. Nonetheless, it's not for the long-limbed European. The process is cursory and haphazard and he's up hanging the shirt in no time.

'How did I do?' He holds up the hanger to show me.

'I say well done.' In spite of everything, it makes me smile. It's a glimpse of what we used to have.

'Do you have any plans today?'

'I'm going to Kagurazaka,' I say quickly, in case he thinks I'm going to cling on to him until I leave Tokyo. 'I'll be out in a few minutes.'

'What's in Kagurazaka?'

'A café.' I have resolved to find the mysterious New Zealand coffee shop. He may know or may be able to help me find it, but I don't bother to ask or divulge more information than necessary. After all, I feel like he doesn't really care. He doesn't show any concern about my visa. He has no desire to know me deeply. He doesn't ask anything about me or my family.

Sometimes I wonder how someone so concerned about the world's big issues – talking about government surveillance, 'occupying Wall Street' and reposting self-righteous op-eds – can be so indifferent to people he actually knows. While I engage him, to some extent, in these draining discussions, I can't get into them because it's all so idealistic. Until I turned thirty, I was that person, but then I grew up and realised that however romantic and radical a revolution sounds – summed up in a word, a catchphrase or iconography that you can put up as a poster in a dorm room or post as a trending hashtag or meme – it's not realistic. I know how it is because I've been there before. I went through one in 1986. All the changes won't happen overnight because of the electric frenzy of a single rally. And yet, here I am, guilty of believing in the same principle when it comes to love and relationships.

What did I want to happen here? I know I'm acting on my innermost impulses, but I do wonder why he's allowed me to see all this. I could have come much, much later, even in the dead of night when his fabulous party was over, so he could spend as little time as possible with me. How quickly things have changed in a matter of days. We now move within a strange dynamic wherein I want to be with him but I'm somewhat resentful of him. He asks me to come as soon as I can, and after I do, he's cold and distant. Why agree to it at all? Why not just say no?

It crosses my mind that he might actually like my company. But he can't possibly. *The ceiling.* If on the off-chance he does, would it hurt to show enthusiasm as I have shown him? I have yet to see any evidence of that. Is he being polite? Does he feel obliged to accommodate me? I'm not simply here for convenience. I did make it clear I wanted to make the most of my remaining time. I really do wish to spend it with him.

'I'll have to give you this key. In case you need to come back earlier.' He hands me a key with no key ring. It's a far cry from his previous behaviour with his apartment. 'You're welcome to visit my tiny studio,' he had said in January when I was planning my trip. And when I asked him how long he could put me up, he said his landlord had issues with tenants having guests. And thus, Garden View. Later, I'd realised that he had said *visit* rather than *stay*, and I was embarrassed for myself. Granted, at the time we'd only been together for one night and I could've turned out to be a complete nut job. But since I've arrived, I've been to his apartment three times, and now I'm sleeping over. Surely he must like me or trust me somehow? He has dispensed with any attempt at furtiveness, which means it never really was about the landlord.

I get myself ready to leave for Kagurazaka.

'Which way are you going?'

'I have to take the train at Sasazuka.'

'I'll go out with you. I'm headed that way.'

Landon hangs on as if awaiting more information about my plan, while at the same time coming across as indifferent. He's being a difficult read. He did say he had a party to go to, so I find no need to disclose any more. I thought he'd be leaving much later, but he gets dressed, wearing the freshly ironed shirt and a pair of black jeans. At the door, we put on our shoes. On the balcony, he unchains his bicycle from the banister and together we head downstairs. Once we're through the low gate, I head on without him, thinking he'll be riding his bicycle anyway.

'Wait for me!' Landon says. I stop momentarily so he can catch up. He walks his bike with me to the end of the alley, all of a hundred steps. I don't get it. I don't see what for. Is he enjoying the torture? Is he enjoying baiting me with himself? Dangling himself but denying me the satisfaction? It seems odd not to be talking, and I detest small talk. I have no choice, however.

'So what party is this?'

'For a friend of mine. It's his birthday.'

Or is it yours?

We reach a highway, the size of which catches me by surprise. 'Looks like I need to cross this,' I say. He stares at me in such a solemn way, as if he's about to say something. I wonder if he's hoping I'll ask him to join me in Kagurazaka. Maybe he does want to be asked, only to reject me. That's probably what he would love to do as a self-assurance of his power over me. In the end my fear of another rejection is too great to surmount, and I don't ask him.

If you want to come, go ahead and ask me. Please ask me.

'Have fun at the party,' I say.

He has not broken his stare. A spark of worry flickers in me, and the roaring sound of the highway seems suddenly louder. Finally, he hops onto his bike and cycles away towards Yoyogi-Uehara. I watch him momentarily and a small yet heavy part of me is remorseful for letting him go. I quash it immediately. He had not wanted to come to the hanami. He had not wanted to go out on his birthday. He

158

will not visit me in Manila. I asked to stay with him because here in Tokyo I know that's my happiest place. Is this it? Is this as good as it gets? I hope tomorrow's a better day. It better be a better day.

I look ahead. The light changes. The speedy traffic stops momentarily, and I cross the highway. I see a sign that says 'Ohara'. On the other side, I continue along the quiet and tapering streets. Ohara doesn't look any different from Shimokitazawa. Every now and then I see the familiar outlets and small neighbourhood shops. According to the map, Sasazuka station shouldn't be far. I should get there soon. But I've never taken this route before, and it always feels further the first time.

Chapter Fourteen

I've definitely seen more forbidding stations than Sasazuka and yet the feelings of emptiness and alienation still loom large. What have I accomplished on this trip? Perhaps it won't be discernible until I see it from a distance, when I'm looking down at the city from the plane. I tell myself to find this café to get a sense of purpose, that maybe by finding it I'll have succeeded in something.

Despite my thorough research, I never found an exact address, only directions from a bad translation. Despite great advances in technology, East-to-West online translation leaves something to be desired. I find translation from European languages excellent, but with its own alphabet, Japanese translations are quite something. I see a phrase only four characters long and it translates to 'is the one who is the one who is the one who'. I wish myself the best of luck.

I suppose I could've asked Sayumi for accuracy, but I'm so deep into it that this search has become a personal crusade. In some way I rejoice that not everything in Tokyo is mapped out, tagged or available on Street View for all the world to see, and that there are places one has to discover and experience in real life.

I get to Kagurazaka with no problem. I start my quest uphill on Kagurazaka-dori, past now-familiar shops, the Sushi-Go-Round and the hat store where, against all odds, I managed to purchase a hat last summer. I walk down the narrowest of alleys in search of the café, finding interesting restaurants and bars along the way. After about an hour or so I'm back where I started. I have begun to doubt myself and believe that I'm never going to find it. Maybe I should ask for help from a local, or because it's my last day, forgo it until next time. I don't even know when that will be.

I give up and go down the hill to Canal Café for a break. It's no longer outdoor weather, and the late afternoon has the sun hiding over Kagurazaka. Nonetheless, I ask for a table by the water, and thankfully the heating lamps are on. The grey skies and ever-shedding and fading sakura petals cut for the first time a somewhat bleak scene. The symbolism isn't lost on me.

I tell myself, when I finish my coffee, to simply have a leisurely stroll along Kagurazaka-dori free from pressure and expectations. The sun is about to set, and from the bottom of the street looking up, the buildings on both sides form a gorge of lights, framing the sun's purple and orange trails. Slender trees stick out from the narrow sidewalk. I don't know what they are but this late in the spring, they are as bare as in winter.

I reach the top of the hill and the shops peter out. The buildings look more like offices and there's a considerable shift in vibe. I've never ventured this far up. I come across a street on my right that creates a T-junction with Kagurazaka-dori, and on the corner is a Family Mart. My heart skips a beat, but when I turn on the street, I find that it's way too short to be what was described. At the end of this short street, I see a torii gate with tall trees behind it. If there's anything I know for certain in this city, if there's a torii, there must be a shrine. Though I know I've seen countless of them already, my instincts tell me to investigate. I take that street, and indeed, no coffee shop. I've totally given up and decide to explore what's beyond the gate. I reach the torii and it turns out to be right at the intersection of yet another T-junction. The gate marks the beginning of a path lined with lanterns and budding trees. Near the shrine, the atmosphere is instantly subdued.

A few steps from the gate is the chozuya, a pavilion where worshippers perform the temizu, the ritual of washing one's hands and mouth before prayers. Sayumi had taught me the ritual when she took me to the Meiji shrine, so I go ahead and pick up a ladle with my right hand and trickle water through my left fingers. I switch hands and do the same again. Once I'm done, I dribble some water on to my lips using my left hand. I'm no Shinto or Buddhist, nor do I practise any kind of religion, but it's amazing how a simple ceremony can instantly summon, if not your inner peace, your inner calm. When I reach the foot of the steps that will take me up to the shrine, I feel somehow receptive. Of what, I'm not quite sure.

A steady trickle of people climb the wide, stone steps, divided into three sections by spacious landings. There's something different about this shrine. Reaching the space at the top, there's a sense of openness and escape from the claustrophobic density of the city. The entire complex is very well designed, and even the grey, five-storey building on the right is barely noticeable. It houses a stylish café and an art gallery that somehow don't crowd the space. Everything has a sleek and minimal aesthetic; it might've been recently renovated.

The shrine itself, directly ahead, is a low, square structure with a trapezoidal roof in a muted colour, in contrast to traditional roofs, which are very ornate. The haiden, or the front part of the shrine where prayers are offered, is enclosed in glass allowing one to see what's within. I look in, and even though I've never had a glimpse of the inside of a haiden or have a complete understanding of this religion, I long to pray as everybody else does. I realise I don't know how, for Sayumi's tutorial only went as far as the temizu.

I explore around the shrine, and on the left side of it is a small terrace with a refreshing view of the quiet neighbourhood below. I've missed the sunset, but the colours of the sky are at their utmost saturation. Just below the terrace, there's an enormous cherry tree, and because of the light I struggle to make out if the blossoms are white or pink. I return to the front of the haiden, hoping I can figure out how to pray. A young Japanese woman approaches, and I smile at her and ask, 'Can you teach me how to pray?'

'Yes,' she says, bowing to me repeatedly. She's more than happy to do so despite her initial struggle with English. Standing at the haiden, she asks if I have a coin to spare. I do, and when she throws hers in the wooden, waist-high box, I do the same. She then leads the prayer and I copy her every move. She bows twice, claps twice, then with her eyes closed, whispers a prayer. And now I have to say mine. I close my eyes and realise I never pray.

I stand and yearn and will my wordless prayer out of myself with the faith that somehow, in some form, my heart has spoken for me. We bow together one more time to end the prayer.

'You are very good,' she says with a smile. Together we go down the steps. 'Uh, where you from?'

'I'm from New York. I'm visiting a friend.'

'Oh, very nice.'

'What do you call this place?'

'Akagi,' she says. I wish I could remember her kind face, but the sun has long set, and the grounds are shrouded in the dark end of twilight. At the gate I thank her for her help and say goodbye. 'I hope you have a happy travel,' she says as sincerely as I've ever heard anyone. It almost brings me to tears. I think of the travel she speaks of not as this trip, but what's beyond – the years ahead – wherever they may be. I've been to many churches and other places of worship, but the human connection I've just had is in itself a religious experience.

Back on the street, I look to my right. Next to the torii, where the road forks immediately, is a Lawson. It is, in effect, on a corner. But this can't be it. I'm far off Kagurazaka-dori now, and the alley where the café is has a Family Mart on the corner. Or does it? Suddenly I struggle to remember what I'd read. It's easy to confuse the two. Nevertheless, since the alley goes downhill, I surmise that it must be the neighbourhood I saw from the shrine's terrace. I take the alley where the Lawson is, and go in that direction for a bit, careful to remember my way back. There's a nagging feeling within me, but I've been let down before, so I keep any expectations at bay. Besides, there's hardly any businesses in these twisting alleys. It continues to go downhill, and on a slight bend it comes to an intersection. And there on the far corner, on my right, a vertical sign in black and white: 'Coffee Roastery'.

I stare at it with my mouth open. I've found it. I can't believe it. I got so many things wrong. I assumed so many things to be true. For one, the store isn't a Family Mart but a Lawson. I've just been stupid. Above all, it's further up than I thought it was. I planned around outright misapprehension. And then it occurs to me: the name sounds familiar. *It can't be*, I tell myself. *It can't be.*

The coffee shop is upstairs, and the way to get in is through a door at the side of the building, on a short alley that intersects it. Like a zombie, I head towards the door, but before I go in, I look up the alley. It goes uphill, and at the end of it, behind a cherry tree, I see a gable and a familiar roof. It takes me a few seconds to piece it together, and it is what I think it is. It's the shrine's roof. As I was looking out into the city on the terrace, the café was right below all along.

I open the door and immediately find a spiral staircase that leads me upstairs. There's another door, and when I open it, I'm embraced by the warm fragrance of coffee and the mellifluous sound of foaming milk. I'm here. It isn't too big or busy. On the right is the beautiful wooden bar, shaped like a surfboard only it's three times as long. On the wood-panelled wall behind it, green ceramic cups hang from evenly spaced hooks from floor to ceiling, forming a square grid. In front of the bar are five round tables that can seat two, three if you squeeze it. The small windows overlook the alley, but from outside the interior

166

is hardly visible, and the overall effect is clandestine and exciting. A small, framed clipping in English hangs on the wall between the windows, and it confirms my fear.

'Coffee Roastery opens its third location in Tokyo,' the headline says. Below it reads, 'Popular New Zealand chain invades Japan.' It's an article from a New Zealand magazine.

There's no denying it. It is a chain. I've heard the name before – it's a small chain in Auckland that's gaining some traction with their roasting methods – but the name is so generic I didn't think they'd be in Tokyo. It's my biggest disappointment and most idiotic mistake since I started this coffee thing. I have to laugh at myself for allowing it to affect me too seriously and too personally. I can imagine Tadami saying, 'Just get a dog.' I must ask him to say it for me in Japanese.

But I'm here, and I might as well give it a shot. A table is free, and I take it. At the bar I order what they're famous for – a New Zealand flat white – and a cheesecake made with kabocha, a kind of Japanese squash. Despite this unforeseen revelation, I'm still curious to find out exactly what an authentic flat white is supposed to taste like. Legend has it the Kiwis invented the drink, although Australia also makes the claim. The young female barista brings the cheesecake and the flat white over to me, the foam swirled into the customary shape of a heart. I take a few little sips and. . . I don't know what to make of it.

Perhaps because of my disappointment, my discernment has completely abandoned me. Am I supposed to hate this? Can I judge this objectively? What for? It has failed the first rule. I take another sip, and it could've been, for all I know, a latte from any of the decent coffee shops I've been to. At the very least, it's robust and velvety, maybe even one of the smoothest I've ever had.

I stare at the wall directly in front of me where the cups are hung. The sight of them facing the same way with shadows growing longer the further they are from the lights is oddly calming. I look around, and I have to admit, that yes, despite it being a chain, despite being one of many, this particular spot is indeed wonderful. It's so hidden. Its location so unexpected and hard to find. The atmosphere inside, meanwhile, is for those days when I don't want to know what goes on outside. As I drink more of the coffee with the cheesecake, I start to enjoy being there, in spite of myself. If I were to put this up as a challenge, these hanging cups would be the photo. The clue would be 'a kiwi doesn't fall far from a cherry tree'. But I cannot. I send it to Landon instead. He replies almost instantly.

Coffee Roastery, he says. I'm stunned. *You do know it's a chain, right?*

I don't reply.

I find myself back in Shimokitazawa earlier than I should. For a Sunday night the neighbourhood is just the right amount of lively. After dinner, I stop by the flower shop one last time for a drink. It's a different bartender, and because I don't have the verve to explain what a French 75 is, I ask for a gin and tonic. I admit to myself that I'm shirking from having to face Landon. I don't understand myself. I asked to stay with him so I could see him, and yet I don't want to go back. Now I'm out here when I could've returned to the comforts of Garden View.

What's the matter with me? How do I navigate myself out of all this? I fear that I will see the wood for the trees only when I have left. Though that's in less than a day, it seems a long, long way off. Days ago I feared the end, sad at the image of him walking away from the supermarket even though it was only the beginning, the first morning, fresh, like the dewy oranges we laughed about hanging over a wall. There was such an overwhelming joy I could barely stay in the moment. It's a stark contrast to how I am now, wanting to break away from this cocoon that I've spun around myself. Surely there must be some sense to this madness I've brought upon myself?

I order a second drink and, moments later, surrounded by bouquets, I bawl like a fool. I cry, thinking I may never stop. Eventually I do. I pull myself together before heading back to Landon's. I pay for my drink and walk to his apartment. I find it in total darkness, and I assume he's not home. I turn the light on in the kitchen and hear his voice.

'Come to bed, darling,' he says. I'm surprised he's already there. It's not even that late. I slip out of my clothes and turn the light off. I creep into the bedroom and feel the cold tatami mat under my feet. I climb in next to him and lie to his left, his bad ear. In the darkness I feel his hand touching my hair. He strokes it gently.

'I'm sorry about the café,' he says.

'It's not what I thought it would be. I thought it would be different from the others. Otherwise it was perfect.'

'Maybe it can be perfect in a different way. Maybe you can overlook one rule. What was the second rule again?'

'No one you know knows about it.'

'I knew. Does that count? No one you know knows about me.'

'I'm not. . . I'm not sure.'

He continues to stroke my hair. 'And remind me of the third?' he asks.

I fall asleep, and it's the last thing I remember.

Chapter Fifteen

I t had been autumn in New York when I took the ferry to Greenpoint. After yet another friend moved to this Brooklyn neighbourhood, I thought I'd better take a look at the coffee shop scene in the area. I could have taken the G train, the origin of many commuter tribulations, but the ferry was a much more interesting way of getting there. From Pier 11 in lower Manhattan, the East River ferry cruised up the river and beneath three of the many iconic bridges of the city: Brooklyn, Manhattan and Williamsburg. It took less than an hour. For all the subway's shortcomings, the city does have a gem in the ferry system.

I got off at the Greenpoint landing and walked up a few blocks on India Street. It was late October, and its many trees, despite the warm weather, had already started to turn. Past brick townhouses and stoops, I found myself quickly in the heart of the neighbourhood. A café with a blue and yellow storefront caught my eye. It reminded me of a tatty but charming coffee shop I fell in love with in Crouch End in north London, across from the old church that's now a recording studio.

The floor space was probably slightly bigger than most ground-floor businesses in New York and was also laid out wisely. There were a few choice seats in this café but the best for me was the one at the back of the bar. The bar ended abruptly, leaving an isolated corner with enough room for a red vintage love seat and a low, brass, round table. From the red sofa I could see the last of the tables with armed chairs and a wall of antique frames, which I realised were all empty. Next to the table was a floor lamp with a red shade, and then the doorway to the anteroom. The red lamp and the empty frames were so distinctive, and the light coming from the backyard through the doorway gave it all a sense of intimacy. It was the perfect point of view for the coffee shop challenge, and a good one, too. I took the photo and posted it with the clue 'lone, stray London mammal'.

Of the few photos I received, Landon's was the best. Taken with a professional camera with a slightly wide lens, it was better than mine but still showed the exact point of view, which meant he'd once sat on the red sofa in the corner by himself. Most important of all, he guessed the name of the coffee shop, Odd Fox.

You're the winner, I texted him. *Very impressive.*

We have many foxes in London.

Makes sense a Londoner would guess it.

Used to be. Now I'm a Tokyo resident.

Oh, that's nice. I was just there this summer. Are you staying in Greenpoint while you're in New York?

No, I was visiting a friend who lives in Greenpoint. He happens to follow this account. He thought it looked familiar, but he couldn't crack the clue. He's American, you see.

Ha ha. Yes, we don't have foxes here. We have a healthy population of rats, though.

I like your hair, Landon wrote. He must've seen the staff photos. *Is there a way I can message you privately?*

Intrigued, I gave him my information.

We need to make out at once, was the first thing he said. *Like ten minutes ago.*

Maybe, if I knew what you looked like.

Oh, I'm sorry. He sent me a link to a social media account, and I liked what I saw.

Who do you remind me of?

Every other English guy.

He was probably in his early thirties, but he had a very serious, intense air about him that made him seem older. However, when his teeth showed – not necessarily in a smile – the gap between his two front teeth suddenly took him down to college-age.

You're cute.

You too. You are so my type. Are you sitting in a café somewhere?

No, I'm at our office in Hell's Kitchen.

Walk calmly to your boss. Knock him out with something. Run.

I just missed him. Turns out he left for the day.

Cool, please let me know a good time and place to meet.

I was flattered, and quite intrigued, but I didn't take his request seriously. Meanwhile, I continued to exchange messages to get to know him more. I was curious to know how he'd ended up in Tokyo.

About four years ago I qualified to become an English teacher. I had been living in London at the time and was dismayed by the job market. I looked into opportunities to teach abroad. I thought maybe China, but the job in Japan came about. I thought about

173

it for a couple of months, and by the summer I had moved to Tokyo.

We got on well; he had wit and humour in equal measure. He wanted to meet up but was leaving for Boston for a couple of days. As it happened, I had also been in Boston, in the spring, just before I went to Tokyo.

We're destined to miss each other, I said facetiously.

I'm not a superstitious person but my joke haunted me, and after he came back from Boston, I thought there was no reason why I shouldn't meet him. But it was his turn to be coy, and he couldn't find the time. He'd probably found much more challenging quests to pursue.

I might be all booked up. Sorry to be flaky!

I shrugged and moved on with my life. A couple of days later, he messaged me again.

Hey, what are your plans today?

I'm having lunch with a friend in Tribeca.

I'm leaving tomorrow. Any chance I can see you at some point? I promised a friend to have dinner, but before six and after nine I'd be free.

Sure. I'm working tomorrow so before six would be good.

Great. I'm at MoMA PS1 right now. Do you want to walk the High Line with me? I'd like to check out Chelsea Market, too. Maybe we can have a drink around there?

I won't walk the High Line with you. But I'll meet you at the Chelsea Market.

That afternoon I set off to walk from the East Village to the Meatpacking District. It was now early November, but it still felt far from fall. It was muggy and overcast; a late-season tropical storm had just passed. Little did I know the greyness of that afternoon foreshadowed the greyness of our time in Tokyo. If there was a moment where I could have turned around and walked away, it would have been this. At any point in my walk from the East Village I could've distracted myself and abandoned my plan. I could've loitered in Washington Square Park and listened to impromptu jazz bands from NYU students or found that coffee shop in the West Village that my co-worker Deniece had been telling me about. But in half an hour I found myself on the cobblestone streets of the Meatpacking District, and on Ninth Avenue I stood at the entrance to the market.

Rush hour was about to peak, and the craziness of the market in the late-afternoon hours swept me in as if I had no choice in the matter. The crowd was like a two-way jet stream in a small tunnel, but Landon's blue eyes pierced through the maelstrom. He clocked me no sooner than I had clocked him, and in that moment our eyes met. I knew there was no turning back.

Everything else that night – cocktails under a tree on Tenth Avenue, our walk from the west to the east side of the city, the rally in Union Square and all that time we spent in his hotel room – was pretty much a scumble of colours and images.

Is there something to be guilty about? I've merely exercised my right in an open relationship. If anything, I'd managed to let go. After a long, long while I did something and I was in the moment, and I didn't think and speculate about the consequences before it finished. How different it was that morning, for I opened my eyes to the beautiful and the frightening.

Landon slept deeply and with nary a sound, buried

under the duvet with his head sticking out. As far as I could remember he didn't grind his teeth. He had mentioned wanting to have breakfast with me before heading to the airport, but I let him sleep some more. It was way too early to wake him. I went back to bed and lay next to him. In admiration of his beautiful face in the soft dawn light, in the stillness of the early morning, I noticed a faint scar on his right eyelid.

An hour later, I told him it was time to get up.

He packed his bags and cheeses.

We left the hotel.

We walked down to the café.

We ordered coffee from Danny.

We talked about the coffee shop rules.

Danny came with the coffee.

'I have cat's tongue,' Landon said.

'A cat's what?'

We laughed about it.

We laughed about his relationship with ramen.

We laughed about animals blowing out birthday candles.

'Okay, okay,' he said to bring us to order. 'We were talking about the rules! What is the third rule?'

'Oh, yes. The third rule. It's short-lived. Keeping it to myself doesn't do it any good.'

'Writing about them helps their business, but then everybody comes and spoils the peace.'

'If I find something beautiful and keep it a secret, the business closes.' I couldn't help but feel remorseful all of a sudden. 'Most good things in life are fleeting. Why is that?'

'Because they're just a means to a greater end unbeknown to us,' he said wistfully, his big blue eyes fixed on me.

There really was a genuine sense of regret hanging over us. When it was time to say goodbye, we stood on the corner of 5th Street and Second Avenue, hopeful about this vague idea that we'd see each other again. Neither of us thought it might actually happen. He opened his arms and held me tight, so tight and for so long I sank into him like I'd never emerge again. I didn't want him to let me go, and he knew. He always had that awareness of me, an intuition, that sense of me falling behind on the street.

'Louie,' he whispered. 'I'm somewhat distressed that tomorrow I won't wake up next to you.'

It was, remarkably, the only time I ever heard him say my name. He then held my face with both hands and kissed me before I turned and walked away. I didn't want to fall for him, but god, I really liked him. In my ill-advised attempt to resist, I walked straight to the subway station without looking back, without watching him take a taxi and vanish around the corner. I knew my weaknesses, and if seeing someone off in a yellow cab, in the streets of downtown Manhattan on a New York fall day, can disarm the most guarded and jaded of hearts, then I was a lost cause. By staying on course and fighting the urge to get one last glimpse of him, I thought I had eluded it, but those words were too powerful.

I'm somewhat distressed that tomorrow I won't wake up next to you.

Chapter Sixteen

I *could* stay lying here in bed so he can wake up next to me. The shoji is partly open, and the early-morning light from the small window above the kitchen table creeps into the bedroom. The soft illumination casts a glow in Landon's hair, much like it did a few days ago when he cooked for me. I see the scar on his eyelid, and in this light it's never as faint as I think it is. It's only in this bedroom, through the translucent shoji, that the scar reveals the seriousness of the cycling accident.

I've been waking up so early every day this past week, and my last day in Tokyo is no different. Like my first morning I find him sleeping next to me, but this time he's on his front, his face squished on the pillow and extending his lower lip out. Perhaps because he's face-down, he's not grinding his teeth. I know a few things about him now, and this one I know for sure: he won't be up in a while. He loves a lie-in, but as nostalgic and sentimental as it sounds to stay here so he can wake up next to me, I decide to go out for a walk.

The streets are empty, as they always seem to be in this part of the neighbourhood, but then again, it's still too early for the Monday-morning rush. My cursory exit from

Garden View has been troubling me, so I find myself going back. I still have it until 9 a.m. I sit on the bed and reach to slide the window open. There's the tree. What is it about this tree? It speaks to me and yet I've no clue what it's trying to say. I do wish there was some metaphysical meaning intended for me, but somehow I find that absurd. It's a beautiful tree, that much is true, but at the end of the day it's just like any other tree. It doesn't flower or do any special tricks. It's simply there, looming. A presence. Perhaps there doesn't have to be a profound meaning to it, or anything for that matter. It just is.

I soak it all in, nonetheless. I doubt I'll ever be in Garden View again. I give the studio a once-over for anything I missed yesterday, and notice underneath the kitchen table the box in which the travel book came. It's empty, two flaps sticking up, trimmed with frayed brown packing tape. I pick it up, but when I open the bottom to collapse it, I wonder why it feels like it's my heart I'm hollowing. We waited for it to arrive that afternoon. We lay in bed talking, and I drew on his back. How can I return to that time? With every minute that goes by, I drift further away from it. I can't believe, after the Loft paper bag, another empty vessel has just made me sentimental.

I look closely at the white square sticker on top. It's peppered with Japanese characters, and on the bottom left corner there's a curious symbol of a cat with a kitten in its mouth. I understand nothing except for the words emblazoned in the middle: David James Landon.

Someone once asked me how I could manage the immensity of New York. *How can you take all this?* I had asked myself this question a long time ago, but it was only when I started hunting, when I took long walks and retreated into myself while keeping a constant eye out for that perfect, surreptitious coffee shop, that I realised I coped with New York when I could find the small town within it. Since that dawned on me, I've believed it to be true. 'Town' need not be an entire neighbourhood – it could be a short cross-town block where tourists don't go, or a restaurant or a store that only locals know. They aren't usually, in my experience, in business for very long, but they bestow experience that endures and nurtures. Look for the small town in the big city. I've often wondered if it could hold true elsewhere.

I close the window and give the room one last look before leaving Garden View for good. I take in streets I haven't walked along before now and see the neighbourhood a little differently. A city of 14 million people yet I've come to conclude that I've found it. I've found the small town in this big city.

My street, Café Use – which is always nearly empty (how long will it stay in business?) – the big grocery store with the masked cashiers. And then there's the small bakery I've been frequenting in the mornings. If they renamed it Jet Lag Coffee Shop, I'd approve because it's perfect for it. It's one of the few stores open very early, along with the hardware store that sells cloven rubber boots and other oddities. It sits on the corner of two alleys in an unattractive peach-coloured building. Inside, there's a greasy-spoon vibe to it, and the shelves of bread against the large window frighteningly remind me of a particular Sainsbury's Local in west London. Thankfully, the overall experience is far from depressing. I don't want to return to Landon's too early just to watch him sleep so I have one last breakfast at the bakery.

Afterwards, I'm pleased to see I've got my timing right. When I walk in, Landon is making coffee in his underwear. His hair is gloriously tousled and his blue eyes sunken and bulging at the same time.

'Went out for a walk?' he asks.

'Beautiful day,' I say.

Landon puts a couple of heaped scoops of grounds into a pour-over cup perched on a tall glass carafe. Deliberately, he pours hot water in and instantly it becomes a dark quicksand of bitterness. He gazes intently at the cup as if lasers beamed out of his eyes, his nose pointed like lightning. Once again I wonder if he's angry, even though I know he's probably not. Inscrutable solemnness. The coffee threatens to percolate out into the carafe. Finally, after several tense seconds, the dark goodness drips down slowly into a steady dribble.

He pours me a cup and another for himself. He then steps into the bedroom and puts on a sleeveless shirt and shorts. 'I'm going for a run,' he says, 'while I still have the resolve. Then I'll make us lunch.' He grabs a sweatshirt and dashes out. He seems to have mastered dashing out. At the train station the other day he simply turned around and vanished. Now I find myself sitting alone at the kitchen table drinking coffee and looking at his abandoned cup, still full, still steaming. *I can't handle hot.* On the windowsill I see the Milk Hall postcard I'd given him, and the bright sunlight has made my inscription on the back visible through the front, like the faded graffiti on the walls of the jazz café.

For a moment I think I'm imagining the cacophony of the café, but the sound turns out to be real. For the first time since I arrived in Tokyo, I hear neighbours. The noise sounds too far off to be coming from the apartment next door, but it could be from the next building. Intrigued, I get up to peek through the bedroom window. I'm surprised to find Landon has drawn the curtains. He has let the light in, giving, for the first time, a clearer, brighter look to everything. In the dimness of the past week most of the details were easily overlooked, but in the cold light of day I confront every bit of reality and I'm almost overtaken with emotion.

I make the bed, laying flat the stripy duvet Landon had wrapped around me. On the tatami just outside his closet, I see some of his shirts strewn in a pile, clothes I've only seen him wear in photos he's sent me. It's incredible how much pathos those clothes evoke. For the five months I longed to see him, that was my idea of him. This was the boy I met in New York. This was the boy I looked forward to seeing. This was the boy I planned to rendezvous with. Is he different now after I've grown to know him? Or is he still the same because I know him better?

Then there's the most recent shirt, the grey checkered one he ironed yesterday, labouring on his knees for a party with his allegedly more stylish friends. I pick it up from the pile and place it on a hanger. He doesn't need to improve his wardrobe. In a corner I see a vintage leather bag gathering dust, and I remember the joke about splitting up with a girlfriend for her poor taste in bags. When was that? It was only a week ago and it feels like a decade. How strange that a funny memory can be so melancholy.

Like Garden View, I'll probably never see this apartment again. But I take comfort in knowing that for as long as he lives in this apartment, he'll be here to tie me to this moment, a silent witness to what we had. But if he moves, or finds that house in the suburbs, or leaves Japan for good, how will I be connected to this time and place? Who will attest, at the time the blossoms were in full bloom, to the beauty that also thrived here? To him this will probably be just a fleeting memory. I, on the other hand, will remember everything, from the most shameful of emotions to those that made me feel alive. I'll remember the most insignificant details, how he comes back from running, how he takes off his shirt, how a drop of sweat from behind his bad ear rolls slowly, uniting with other beads that gently run down his back. How he catches his breath, how he mumbles something about his heart rate, how proudly he says, 'All before breakfast.'

He jumps in the shower and comes out in the giant blue towel that he's been sharing with me. I admire his naked body, in a non-lascivious way, for the last time. I'm saddened that this thing between us – between two people when they are young, lithe and beautiful – may never happen again. Life is so short, that much is true, but youth is even briefer. We barely get the chance for anything. I've never thought of myself as old, but for the first time I feel like I've crossed the borders of youth.

As promised, he does make a big effort cooking our lunch. It's a Korean frittata, I think I hear him say, but I can't be sure. I help him chop potatoes. 'Cut them this way,' he says. And even though he thinks I have inferior knife skills because of my left-handedness, I don't say anything, because I want him to take control of me. For one last time, I want him to have his way with me, as easily as the two fistfuls of greens wilting in the pan. I watch him cook with such focus, pouring the eggs very carefully to a gentle sizzle.

It hits me: he may not be as demonstrative as I wish him to be in all other respects, but in cooking for me I can see how much he cares. Now I know he does this for both of us, for our enjoyment, like all the meals he's made. He has always made sure I get a beautiful meal.

In the flipping stage, however, the frittata shatters into several pieces. He's clearly disappointed, and mutters something about the spatula. The tragedy breaks my heart. I want him to succeed. I smile encouragingly. I don't want him to think he's failed me or that I think less of him because our final meal is less than perfect.

'I ruined it,' he says, serving the dish.

'I'm sure it's no less delicious.'

He sits next to me as usual. 'Itadakimasu,' he says. We eat on the same plate as we've always done, and I almost lose it. I can't figure out if I'm sad because I'm leaving, or because I'm leaving and he doesn't seem to be sad. Like everything he's cooked, it's superb.

'I owe you a lot of meals,' I say when we're done.

'Don't worry about it. Sorry you got this guy who makes pretentious crap.'

'Is that what you think I think?' I say reflexively. I can tell he's faintly taken aback by my sudden, although minor, outburst. 'I want you to know I appreciate everything. I owe you a night, too. Should you ever be in New York again, or find yourself in Manila. . .'

He doesn't utter a word. He's as silent as the cold coffee in front of him.

I get up to retrieve my bags in the bedroom. I had thought about this beforehand, ultimately deciding to go ahead with it not because I want to hurt him, but because I don't want to hurt myself. I can't keep a physical reminder of him.

'I'd like to give this back.' I hand him the travel book.

'No, please,' he says, visibly dismayed. 'Please keep it. It's yours.'

'I really appreciate it, but I've no need for it. It would be more useful to someone else. You could give it to another visiting friend.' As I say these words I hope I don't come across as vengeful or bitter, and I certainly don't mean to insinuate or cast aspersions on future guests. When Landon's hand meets the book, I'm instantly filled with remorse. *Have I made a mistake?* I know that if I keep that book, it will sit on a shelf with no purpose other than to remind me of him. Even though he avoids making eye contact I can see the disappointment and sorrow in his eyes, and the last thing I want to do is cause him pain.

'Are you flying from Narita?'

I nod. 'The express leaves Shibuya in about an hour.'

'You can take a car from here to Shibuya. Do you want me to call one?'

'No, it's fine. I still have plenty on the Pasmo.'

'I'll walk with you then.'

He'll walk with me to the station and, after saying goodbye, I'll go through the turnstile and watch him turn around and walk away. He'll walk away back into Shimokitazawa, the neighbourhood I've come to love,

186

onto its streets, into the crowd, amid the craziness, under a storm of signage. I'll watch him get smaller and smaller and I'll stare as much as I can to hold sight of him until I can no longer see him. It will be too much for me, and I will break. It is I who should walk away. I'd rather leave him like this, here in this apartment, and when I think of him this will be my memory of us. Should he move cities, countries or continents, I'll still think of him here, in the quietness of this room, in this dreamy, perpetual greyness, cooking a meal and eating from the same plate as the explosion of cherry blossom takes place outside. I do hope I will have the answer when I ask myself in the future if he ever thinks of me too. Will he remember me when he walks by the quiet café or the strange supermarket? Will he keep that postcard on the sill until sunlight bleaches the image of the jazz café? Will he finally gaze long enough at the photo I took of him and see that in his clear-blue eyes he'll find a reflection of me?

'It's okay,' I tell him. 'I'll walk by myself.' I put my jacket on and hang my bags over my shoulders. He opens the door for me, and we stand in the hallway. 'Take care,' he says. He gives me a peck on the lips.

'Goodbye.'

He shuts the door and I make my way downstairs, out of the confines of the tiny apartment. I squint to adjust to the brightness of the afternoon, but the hurt in his eyes when I handed him back the book remains in my mind. Could it be? Could it be possible he shares my feelings after all? That the absence of sadness on my departure is nothing but pretence? I never found the right moment nor the temerity to speak from the heart. Somehow that doesn't matter now. We may never see each other again. I simply need to say the words. I can come out of this without a shred of dignity, or I can come out of this without regret. I decide which is more important of the two, and which I can bear to live with like a disfiguring scar. I put my bags down at the foot of the stairs and climb back up the steps. I gently open the door to his room, and he's washing up at the sink. The water is running, and he doesn't hear me.

'Landon,' I call out to him. He turns to me, perplexed as to why I'm back at his door. 'I love you.'

The words come out of my mouth like a bird in a precarious stance, its wings beating mightily to gain the certainty of flight. Time slows down momentarily, and I see clearly the exact moment those words perch in his ear. He blinks, and his eyes betray the truth of what he thinks of them. Before I can even begin to brace myself for what's to come, he laughs mockingly out of his nose like I'm some random, ridiculous fan. Without a word he turns his back to me and carries on with the dishes, indifferent to my presence, having no doubt that, sooner or later, this annoyance, this – what did he call me? – limpet, will leave him be. It's a pure and inexpressible devastation within me, a mushroom cloud within my chest, and I should feel divinely blessed that he doesn't see my face. I retreat and close the door behind me. I head down the stairs and pick up my bags. I go through the small gate and make my way out of the alleyway, turning the corner past the old cherry tree, treading on the carpet of petals it has shed.

Indeed, just as I imagined, there's no redemption from

this, and it's the price I pay for choosing closure over dignity. I emerge onto Kamakura-dori, and trudging towards the station I pass by my street. *You're only ten minutes away from me.* With my bags it seems much longer. At the station, I tap the Pasmo card he had helped me get. *It has enough to last you until the end of your trip.* Indeed it has; I, however, barely hung on. I stand on the platform waiting for the train to Shibuya, and the usual crowds swirl around me. . . .*you didn't go down in a ball of flames.* Well, now I just might.

Landon and I will never speak to each other again. If we do, it will not be for a very long time. I'll think of him at least once a day over the next year or so. He won't know or care about the heartbreak, and how the remnants of it fester and become hate. He won't know how much I'll loathe him for the loathing I have for myself, for allowing all of it to happen. He won't know that every spring I'll fail miserably to forget his birthday. I'll see the odd cherry blossom in New York, and though seemingly alien and out of place, it is a sight to behold. But as quickly as it comes, it withers and dies, just as our time together did. In no time at all there will be no trace of it blooming, and I will manage to put him out of my mind until another spring comes along.

One day, the hate will become a hope that at some point we could be friends. I'll want to know how he is – I'll want to share the news that the Australian-Argentinian café on 5th Street has gone out of business at the end of one summer, boarded up like many businesses in New York, doomed both by the pandemic and looting – but I'll stop myself from reaching out to him. I'll walk around the city, now more anonymous with everyone wearing face masks, as if the cashiers of the Japanese supermarket have invaded New York. I'll make eye contact with a masked man with blue eyes and invisible eyelashes, and for a split second I'll think it's him. But I'll be certain it could not be him, for even after all that time the exceptional intensity of his eyes is simply something I can never forget.

I get to Shibuya a lot earlier than planned, but it's just as well. Judging by the number of people on the platform, it looks like it's going be a full train. Of the three times I've taken the express, none of them were ever this busy. This will not be the quiet ride I had hoped for, with nearly empty cars. The express finally arrives, shiny and jaunty like a toy. I find myself, like everybody, clustering at the doors. Most of us are non-Japanese and the absence of the order I've grown accustomed to throws me off. Checking my ticket, I find my seat by the window near the front of the car. The train won't leave for another five minutes, and the feeling of consternation rises inside me as people crowd the aisle and the seats get filled. I'm plunged back into the world, and it's at that moment that I feel how isolated and detached I've been these last seven days.

A few minutes later, I hear an announcement in Japanese and English that the train is departing. The doors close with an airtight pneumatic hiss, and I feel a gentle lurch when the train slowly pulls out of the station. I look out the window. The slow parade of utility poles and repeating shapes of slack powerlines lulls me into exhaustion. Suddenly I feel all the emotions catch up with me, but I hold them in. I don't want to cry here. In the row ahead, a couple of young American tourists chatter boisterously with their friend who sits next to me. While some peace would be welcome, I'm grateful to hear a familiar sound from a familiar world that, as the train gets up to full speed, blurs this one I'm leaving behind. This place, this time, this love, flourish – and vanish – all together.

Book Club Questions

Louie has three rules for the perfect coffee shop: One, it's one of a kind. Two, no one you know knows about it. Three, it's short-lived. How do these rules manifest in other parts of his life? And how can he break free from them?

The anxiety around Louie's visa is an important thread in his story, contrasted with Landon's British passport that allows him more freedom of movement. In what way do you think this might affect their relationship?

The narrative switches between spring in Tokyo and autumn in New York; each place is distinct from the other, as though they are their own characters. What role do both these cities and seasons play in Louie's life?

Louie is a tourist in Japan and naturally spends his time getting lost while eagerly exploring the city. How does this contribute to the atmosphere of the novel, his sense of belonging and his assuredness in his relationship?

Louie eats ramen alone when he first lands in Tokyo, Landon cooks him sunny-side-up eggs, Sayumi takes him out for tonkatsu and he bonds with Sebastian over burgers. Do these foods say anything about Louie's moods or his relationships?

Landon gifts Louie a book when he first arrives, Louie gifts Landon a postcard before he leaves. How do these gifts convey each character's intention towards the other? And what else, beyond these physical items, do they give to each other?

Sayumi and Sebastian offer salvation to Louie while he's in Tokyo, he speaks to them both about their relationships to reflect on his own. Why do you think he didn't tell them about Landon, and do you think it was the right decision?

The romance between Louie and Landon feels push and pull, on and off. Louie doubts how much Landon likes him, while Landon gives mixed signals. How invested in their relationship do you think Landon is?

Do you think Louie and Gabriel or Sayumi and Takemi stay together? What do you think Landon's future relationships be like? Will Sebastian keep one of his relationships or continue to keep both?

According to the attachment theory on relationships, there are four attachment styles: Secure, Anxious, Avoidant, Disorganised. Do you think either Landon or Louie fall into a particular type?

Acknowledgements

This book is dedicated to Alex Gifford for his steadfast love and commitment, in and out of my writing sphere.

My road to publishing took many years, and it did not come without its unhealthy share of rejections, such that when I was informed that I had won Unbound Firsts' competition with this novel, I only allowed myself to believe that I would be published when the process unfolded unimpeded.

The pieces of the puzzle came together so effortlessly, and when I saw with my own eyes that the people working tirelessly for the success of the book were, in fact, real, I admitted its birth was undeniable.

They've made my life-changing journey as a debut author fulfilling and affecting, thrilling and delightful, all at the same time. To the following, I am deeply grateful:

Sara O'Keeffe, whose persistence in finding a home for this book has transformed me fundamentally.

Kathryn Court for her counsel in the field of publishing through the years.

Amy V. Borg, who saw the beauty in an early version and precipitated a wonderful chain of events.

At Unbound, my editor Aliya Gulamani for championing debut writers of colour. I'm proud to be one of Unbound Firsts' authors.

My editor Marissa Constantinou, who steers every stage of the process. I could not have wished for a more brilliant editor to work with.

The indefatigable team at Unbound: Gemma Davis, Kate Neilan, Ilona Chavasse, Rina Gill, Sophia Cerullo. It's a privilege to be part of a team that works with so much passion.

Mark Ecob for his art direction and Shiori Fujioka for her illustration of the cover.

Rachel Ware and our consequential summer of 2018.

J Flores Beckett, Badj Galias-Genato, Maia Joven, Samara Naier, Victoria Perlas and Rachel Ware for reading early versions. Your feedback is truly appreciated.

Oliver Beigel, Kazumi Kudo, Dexter Fabian, to whom my gratitude will be self-explanatory.

Toby Thompson, poet extraordinaire and ping-pong champion.

The London support team: Jane Gifford & Jamie Telford at FPHQ, Michael Thomas at Sheridans, Tom Lloyd-Williams at ACM UK.

Social media strategy and host of milestone celebrations, Melanie Cuevas.

Miscellaneous thanks to Mina Peralta.

For their participation on social media, who, at the time of this writing, are Iqbal Hussain, Jane Gifford, Jemma Kennedy, Toby Thompson, Alex Gifford, Melanie Cuevas,

Daphne Oseña Paez, Alexey Kim and Marisel Polanco. To everyone else who will have obliged, thank you.

I cannot possibly mention everyone who supported me behind the scenes, indirectly and in immeasurable ways. Please know that I am beyond grateful. Until the next book.

unbound FIRSTS

Unbound Firsts is inspired by our mission to discover new voices, fresh talent and amazing stories. We're proud to offer emerging writers of colour the opportunity to be published by an award-winning publishing house and have their stories shared with readers around the world.

There's an Unbound Firsts book for every reader – whether it's a gripping mystery set in underground Moscow, a time-travelling historical fantasy, or a bold multi-generational debut exploring themes of queerness, revolution and Islamic sisterhood.

Perhaps you're after an uplifting read about following your heart against all odds or are yearning to be transported to Tokyo during cherry blossom season. A contemporary family saga which cleverly blends the laws of quantum physics with everyday suburban life completes the collection.

Unbound Firsts is a celebration of new writing for readers everywhere.

Discover the full collection and dive into your next read today.

Unbound Firsts 🔍

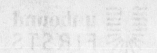

Note on the Type

The text of this book is set in Bembo. Created by Mono-type in 1928-1929, Bembo is a member of the old style of serif fonts that date back to 1465. Its regular, roman style is based on a design cut around 1495 by Francesco Griffo for Venetian printer Aldus Manutius, sometimes generi-cally called the 'Aldine roman'. Bembo is named for Manutius's first publication with it, a small 1496 book by the poet and cleric Pietro Bembo. The italic is based on work by Giovanni Antonio Tagliente, a calligrapher who worked as a printer in the 1520s, after the time of Manu-tius and Griffo.

Monotype created Bembo during a period of renewed interest in the printing of the Italian Renaissance. It con-tinues to enjoy popularity as an attractive, legible book typeface.